Karin Baine lives in Northern Ireland with her husband, two sons, and her out-of-control notebook collection. Her mother and her grandmother's vast collection of books inspired her love of reading and her dream of becoming a Mills & Boon author. Now she can tell people she has a *proper* job! You can follow Karin on Twitter, @karinbaine1, or visit her website for the latest news—karinbaine.com.

Also by **Karin Baine**

The Doctor's Forbidden Fling
The Courage to Love Her Army Doc
Falling for the Foster Mum
Reforming the Playboy
Their Mistletoe Baby
From Fling to Wedding Ring
Midwife Under the Mistletoe
The Single Dad's Proposal
Their One-Night Twin Surprise
Their One-Night Christmas Gift

Discover more at millsandboon.co.uk.

HEALED BY THEIR UNEXPECTED FAMILY

KARIN BAINE

MILLS & BOON

First published in Great Britain 2020
by Mills & Boon, an imprint of HarperCollins*Publishers*
1 London Bridge Street, London, SE1 9GF

Large Print edition 2020

© 2020 Karin Baine

ISBN: 978-0-263-08579-2

For Georgia and Jordan xx

CHAPTER ONE

'SO, YOU'RE THE woman I'm about to impregnate? Nice to see you again.'

'Hello, Mr Garrett.' Kayla O'Connell shook hands with the man her brother, Liam, and his husband, Tom, had set her up with for this baby-making exercise.

So much for this remaining nothing more than a business transaction when one firm handshake, one touch from him was enough to make her weak at the knees. She would rather not have him involved in this at all. It would have been easier to do it with a stranger. Meeting Jamie at her brother's wedding had been sufficient to rattle her.

'Oh, Kayla, I would've thought we were on first-name terms by now. Jamie's fine.'

Even though his slow, sexy smile had her transfixed, that smooth charm he possessed always made her nervous. It reminded her of her parents and the façade they'd used to put on for the rest of the world to hide the multitude of sins committed behind closed doors. He was easy on the eye, but he knew it, and took way too much enjoyment in the fact she blushed every time he came near her.

However, since he was Tom's big brother there was no way of avoiding him. 'Thanks for coming, Jamie.'

'You know I'd do anything you asked. All you have to do is give me the word.' He held her gaze a second longer than necessary, sending shivers all over her body at the underlying suggestion. What scared her more than Jamie's blatant flirting with her was her reaction to it. But rather than admonishing him for his suggestive comments, she had to use all her strength not to give into the temptation he embodied.

'We're not doing this for me. It's for our brothers and that's who we should be focusing on.' Kayla couldn't take her eyes off him as he sat down in the chair opposite, loosened his navy and silver striped tie and undid the top button on his shirt, revealing that small patch of skin at his throat. The picture in her mind took on a whole new explicit nature, transporting the scene into a bedroom rather than a busy London café.

Clearly, her body had gone into panic mode about this surrogacy idea if she was fantasising about the father-to-be. Who, in ordinary circumstances, she would've run a mile from. Lately, she'd gone for safe guys, who never really lit her fire but she knew would never hurt her. Self-preservation after abusive parents and an ex-boyfriend who'd thought he could control her. Thank goodness she'd had her brother's support in helping her realise Paul had gradually been taking over, manipulating her into doing what he wanted and leaving her scared to question him.

It had been a blow to realise she'd reverted back to that submissive behaviour she'd employed to keep her parents happy rather than face the consequences. Trust wasn't something she gave easily, and Paul had taken what was left from her.

It was no wonder her relationships since

hadn't lasted, because she couldn't bring herself to fully invest in them in case history repeated itself. She'd been content being single and not having to worry about anyone except herself. Kayla would go as far as to say she'd never get into another relationship again and certainly had no inclination towards starting a family of her own. That was why being around Jamie was so difficult. She might be attracted to him, but she also knew he was the type of man capable of breaking hearts. His brother had told her as much.

'Of course, but that doesn't mean we can't enjoy each other's company too, does it?' He reached across the table to take her hand and stroked his thumb across her fingers. She could only watch, dumbstruck, knowing she couldn't give an answer without incriminating herself.

A shuffling by the table alerted her to someone else bewitched by her companion. The young girl carrying over his coffee hovered long after she'd set the cup down, openly staring at him.

'Thank you.' He turned on a full-watt grin

that sent the waitress scurrying away again with a giggle. Jamie had that cheeky glint in his brown eyes Kayla was sure made most women swoon, although she knew he wasn't the settling-down type either. That was one of the reasons he'd apparently agreed to do this. Kayla directed her thoughts back to the surrogacy, since that was the reason they were actually here.

'So, I know you're a respected GP in your practice, a partner. Tom told me you raised him after your parents both died, and you've said yourself you don't want anything to do with this baby when it arrives.' It wasn't important how hot his skin felt against hers or that he'd ignored every other woman at the wedding, trying to capture her attention. For these purposes, all she needed to know was that he had brains as well as good looks and that he wouldn't be hanging around driving her to distraction once his part of the deal was over.

'That's not as brutal as it seems on the surface. I'm happy to help the newly-weds start a family but I'm not interested in being a father myself. I don't mind being the fun uncle, though. Do you have a problem with that?' He cocked his head to one side, eyebrow raised as he tried to rile her. She wasn't going to rise to it. Even if he was making sexy eyes at her, causing her to tingle in all sorts of places. Yes, she did have a problem with it.

Perhaps this had been a bad idea, but she'd thought they should at least discuss what they expected from this arrangement. In Jamie's case, apparently that was nothing. He was primarily going to be the sperm donor. Perhaps with the odd appearance for birthdays and family get-togethers.

She couldn't criticise when that was as involved as she wished to be in the baby's life too. In her case, a loving auntie who was free to come and go as she chose. She was the surrogate, an incubator only for this baby, because any idea of family beyond her brother terrified the life out of her. Their parents' tyranny had made her realise the damage a person could do to a child and she didn't want that level of responsibility. Liam and Tom were two of the nicest men on earth and a child would be lucky to have them as parents.

'Not at all. I was just checking.' She sipped her herbal tea and wished the others would hurry up and join them to ease the tension.

She tried to forget their first meeting and how flustered she'd been around him. A matter he'd taken great satisfaction in and flirted with her outrageously until she'd demanded he stop. He obviously wasn't used to women saying no to him, her request amusing him all the more. The truth was she'd been afraid of reacting to his advances when her body had been on fire for him after just a few suggestive comments. He wasn't her type. Actually, she didn't have a type because there wasn't a man alive she was willing to trust.

Of course, their brothers had been blissfully unaware of their sizzling chemistry, so wrapped up in the happiness of their big day. When they'd proposed Jamie as the sperm donor for the surrogate baby she had agreed to carry for them, she'd been unable to find it in her to object to the idea.

'I never thought my little brother would be

the first to get married and have a family.' He shook his head, the affection for his sibling shining brightly in his smile.

'It was a lovely wedding.' The grooms had spared no expense in sharing their happy day with their friends. They'd taken their vows in the Royal Observatory in Greenwich. Toasted with champagne in the courtyard over the Meridian Line, where the east and west hemispheres met. Later, they'd had their meal in the Octagon Room under the stars. Those still standing had gone on to party in a nearby hotel, and booked rooms for the night. The whole day had been magical.

'Amazing. I had concerns it might be a bit… cheesy but I suppose some might have called it romantic.' He leaned across the table as he said it, reminding her of the telescope viewing she'd done with Jamie right there beside her. With him so close she'd been oblivious to anyone else in the room.

As the grooms' family, they'd spent the majority of the day in close proximity but that was the moment she'd become *aware* of him. By that time of the evening, his perfectly groomed hair had had its curl back and he'd had a shadow of a beard bristling over his once clean-shaven jaw. He'd shed his tux jacket and untied his bow tie so it hung loosely around his neck. It wouldn't have taken much to tug on the ends and pull him in for a kiss. One she'd known would be hot when he'd been giving her his undivided attention all day. Thank goodness that had been the moment Tom and Liam had announced they were moving the party to the hotel and saved her from herself.

'The food was good too.'

'The first dance was my particular highlight.' Clearly, he wasn't going to let her forget their more intimate moments of the day.

That first dance, when Jamie had swept her up on the dance floor at the happy couple's insistence they join them, had indeed been memorable. Those three or four minutes in his arms, their bodies pressed close together swaying in time to the music, had been heavenly. When he'd whispered in her ear, asked if she wanted to come up to his room, she'd almost agreed. Her hormones would've followed him across the dance floor and into his bed, but her head and her wounded heart wouldn't allow it. That was when she'd known she'd had to stop his flirting with her and once the song had ended, she'd made sure to keep her distance from him. Until now.

'It was good to see Tom and Liam so in love. They're going to make great parents.'

Jamie sighed, perhaps resigning himself to the fact she didn't want to be reminded of the chemistry they'd experienced that night. Something which apparently hadn't dissipated since they'd last seen each other.

'Tell me, Kayla, what is it you're hoping to achieve by offering yourself up as a surrogate? You're a midwife, aren't you? Surely this isn't a situation you would usually encourage?' He lounged back in his chair, crossed his long legs at the ankles and made himself comfortable whilst he turned the spotlight back on her. It was a safer topic of conversation for her than the wedding night.

'I'm a doula now. I left my position as a midwife so I could give more support to my expectant mothers. It's none of my business what the story behind their pregnancy is but it is my job to be supportive of their choices. I just want parents and babies to be happy. The same goes in this instance too.' She would move in with the guys for the duration of the pregnancy, to keep them involved throughout, then hand over the baby so they could start their happy little family. Something she and Liam had missed out on their entire lives.

'Do you have a problem with that?' Her brother's sexuality was a touchy subject for her and she was very protective of him despite being the younger of the two.

It had been their parents' reaction to him coming out as gay which had finally given her the push to leave that toxic environment with him and move to London from their small village in Northern Ireland. They'd spent their entire childhoods cowed in fear of their disciplinarian parents, but it was when their mother and father had disowned their own son she'd seen them for the monsters they really were.

Jamie set his coffee cup back on the table and held his hands up. 'Not at all.'

'Good. Then we're both on the same page.' This baby was going to share the traits of both its parents and she wanted to be certain there weren't some dodgy conscience-free genes about to be introduced.

'I wouldn't do this for just anybody. It's not as though I make weekly deposits down at the local sperm bank and get off on the fact there could be dozens of Jamie Juniors running around out there. Tom asked me to do this because he can't and with me as the donor it means he still has a biological connection with the baby. The same way Liam has because you're the egg donor.'

'I have my own reasons for agreeing.' Liam deserved to have some happiness and though she hadn't been able to do anything in the past to help, she was in a position to do it now. It was information Jamie didn't need to know. Her past was none of his business.

'Oh? You're not doing it simply out of the goodness of your heart, then? Like me?' He was making fun of her because she was taking this seriously. She wished he would. It would make her feel better to know the father of this baby was sensible, reliable and stable. Even if he wasn't going to be an active participant.

'If you just wanted to have a kid, you should've taken me up on my offer at the hotel.' The man winking at her, and setting her body aflame with desire, didn't fit in with the profile supplied by those who knew him better than her.

From the glowing accounts she'd heard before they'd met, she'd expected a deadly serious, old-beyond-his-years father figure, who'd raised Tom as his own son and was giving him away at the wedding. She'd known he wasn't keen on long-term relationships, but she'd put that down to his busy work schedule. After getting to know him she wondered if there was anything more to him than a rakish playboy who thought nothing of propositioning her. Either way, she'd be having words with her brother about his suitability for this role.

'Don't think it hasn't crossed my mind.' The truth slipped out before she could catch it. She took another sip of her tea to keep her from saying anything else to feed his widening grin.

It wasn't that she'd never been in the company of a handsome man before, or had one come on to her. She'd been getting better at handling herself in those situations because she was sick of pretending to be someone she wasn't. Her early years had been spent trying to be the perfect daughter to prevent angering her parents. The hangover of that learned behaviour as an adult had seen her enter into a disastrous relationship where she'd spent most of it trying, and failing, to meet her partner's expectations. She was done trying and didn't need the drama of having another man in her life. If only all her other body parts agreed with her brain.

'Well now, wouldn't it make more sense to cut out all the intrusive medical procedures and do things the old-fashioned way?'

Now her head was filled with explicit images of Jamie naked except for the tangled sheets they were entwined in. That longing that she'd convinced herself had been a one-off the last time they'd met began again inside her.

With those brown eyes sparkling with mischief and promise, she was tempted to take him up on the offer. Neither of them wanted some grand love affair but it was obvious they had a connection that would make sparks fly.

'I suspect sense wouldn't be playing a big part in that scenario. More like lust.' One of them had to be honest about this attraction they were dancing around. Pretending that this talk of a secret liaison was for their brothers' benefit wasn't fooling anyone.

She swallowed hard and tried to pull herself together. When this pre-conception meeting had been first suggested, she'd sworn not to let him literally charm the pants totally off her this time. Now she was swearing at herself for getting caught under his spell again.

'Would that really be so bad?' His dark gaze rendered her immobile now that he'd made her so hot she'd melted into her chair.

'There's no guarantee we'd conceive that way.' She was scrabbling for excuses now when her head was full of the possibilities available to her with him. The alternative conception method Jamie was suggesting sounded so much more enjoyable than the one planned that she was afraid she was going to take him up on it.

'It doesn't have to be a one-time offer. I'm prepared to put the hard work in to make this happen.' His voice dropped so low she could feel it deep in the pit of her stomach, and lower...

'I, uh...' She had no words. Her brain was mush, her mouth dry. It had been a while since she'd shared a bed with anyone. Longer still since she'd had this level of passion stirred up inside her.

Despite all the promises she'd made to herself about staying away from men, and this one in particular, all she could think about was grabbing him by the hand and finding the nearest hotel room. At this stage she wasn't even thinking of a baby, only her own pleasure. That wasn't part of the deal.

Jamie couldn't believe she was considering his outrageous proposal, or that he'd made it. There was something about Kayla that intrigued him and made him want to push her buttons. When he'd first spotted her at the wedding, he'd known this was the sister Liam had spoken about fondly. The pretty blonde in the off-the-shoulder, gypsy-style floral dress had to be the woman he'd heard loved animals too much to eat them and enjoyed nothing more than meditating and clearing something called chakras. From a distance, she'd seemed so calm and serene and totally in character with the Kayla who'd been described to him. Until she'd spoken to him. Then the carefree, laid-back, spiritual doula he'd heard about had changed into a tightly wound spitfire.

Only around him though, he'd noted. From a distance he'd watched her charm everyone else with her easygoing nature and was amused by her reaction when he was around. Her pale skin flushed a dramatic scarlet when he spoke to her and she couldn't get away from him quickly enough. He might have taken offence if it weren't for the surreptitious glances he noticed she kept shooting his way. Her interest in him seemed to mark a change in his behaviour too. Ordinarily he wasn't quite so…abrasive.

Now she appeared more open to the idea of a fling his juices were flowing. When the air between them was still so charged with sexual awareness in the middle of a coffee shop, he knew they could set the sheets on fire together.

'You know, my place isn't far from here and my car's just outside…' he tossed out as he finished his coffee. It was madness, yet that flash of lust he'd seen when he'd mentioned the idea was unmistakable and irresistible. As was the subconscious licking of her lips and toying with her unruly blond hair. All signs she was interested in him. Along with the fact she was yet to tell him where to get off thinking she was the type of woman who'd agree to some afternoon hanky-panky with someone she hardly knew.

'Jamie, I…uh—'

He was expecting her to turn him down, but she set down her cup with trembling hands and was beginning to lift her handbag from the floor as if she was getting ready to go with him. Jamie unhooked his jacket from the back of the chair and dug for his car keys in the pocket. This was the most spontaneous, reckless thing he'd ever done. That included volunteering to be a sperm donor for his infertile brother.

'I'm so glad we caught you two!'

At the sound of Liam's loud Northern Irish voice, they jumped apart. As though they'd literally been caught in the act. Chance would have been a fine thing.

'Actually, we were just leaving.' He held out a hand to help Kayla up but as she glanced between the two men Jamie knew the moment had passed. For now.

'You can't go yet. I've only got here and Tom's on his way. We want to catch up on all the gossip and tell you what's happening at the clinic.' Liam pulled out a chair and invited himself to join them. The couple had been heavily involved in a project out in Vietnam setting up facilities for medical care in impoverished areas of Central Vietnam and it would be rude of them not to stay and listen to their latest news.

Kayla couldn't even meet his eye now, so Jamie had no choice but to sit back down and quell the excitement that had been escalating until his brother-in-law crashed their party.

Tom arrived shortly after. 'Sorry I'm late. The trains are a nightmare as usual. Got held up leaving Victoria Station because of a signal failure or something. What have I missed?'

He gave Jamie a half-hug and kissed Kayla on the cheek before pulling over another chair from a nearby table and squeezing in beside his husband.

'Nothing. Unfortunately,' he mumbled. It was difficult not to sound ticked off when these two had killed the mood and left Kayla glaring at him for saying so.

'Good. Kayla thought we should meet up to discuss any qualms anyone had about the process. Is there anything we should know about?' Tom's question was met only with silence.

They hadn't got around to listing the pros

and cons about the baby idea when they'd been busy flirting up a storm. Kayla didn't strike him as the type who'd stay silent if she had a problem and, since he'd been on board from day one, Jamie didn't see the point in making them sweat.

'Nope. We're ready and willing to get our baby-making on. Where do we sign?' His answer clearly delighted the two men, who grasped each other's hands.

'Kayla? You're the one who'll be doing all the hard work. Now you've had a chance to talk it over with Jamie, are you happy for us to push ahead?' Even Liam sounded nervous about his sister continuing with her commitment and he didn't know Jamie had just propositioned her.

Any hint of sexual attraction towards him seemed to have evaporated since she was still frowning at him for his earlier indiscreet remark. 'Jamie has made it clear he's not the sort of person interested in committing to this beyond his ability to fill a plastic cup. I think you should get that down in writing in case he changes his mind again.'

Wow. He hoped it was sexual frustration causing her to lash out too. If she really believed he was the unreliable, flaky type who'd mess his brother around, she knew nothing about him at all. He'd spent his whole adult life raising and providing for his kid brother. That was why he'd no intention of marrying or having kids of his own any time soon. Now Tom was married and starting a family, Jamie was free of responsibility. He no longer had a dependant to think of with every decision he made, and he didn't think it was selfish of him to want a little quality time for himself.

He couldn't be sure if she'd formed her disapproval of him at the wedding or this afternoon when he'd made a pass at her and hadn't followed through, but it was no longer important. Once he'd done his part behind closed doors he'd walk away with a clear conscience and wouldn't have to set eyes on her again.

If she was as sensitive as she appeared, he'd be better off letting her despise him. There was no point in getting involved with someone who'd read more into a fling than he was willing to give. Jamie had been there, done that, and wasn't in a hurry to repeat the experience. The same could be said about his attitude to fatherhood.

CHAPTER TWO

IT HAD BEEN three months since that dreaded phone call from Jamie, but she could still hear it.

'I'm sorry, Kayla, there's been an accident. Tom, Liam…they didn't make it.'

Her world had fallen apart with those words at a time when she should have been enjoying her pregnancy. She'd conceived on the first attempt, thanks to the assistance at the fertility clinic and not an afternoon of passion with Jamie. With their brothers' well-timed intervention that day, she'd taken back control of her senses and avoided any further one-to-one dealings with Jamie.

The guys had gone over to Vietnam to tie up loose ends on the project they'd been working on out there. As Tom was an architect, and Liam a builder, they'd used their

skills to build a medical centre for an impoverished area they'd visited on their holidays a few years ago. This was supposed to
have been their babymoon, their last trip before they settled down into family life. Heavy
rainfall had caused flooding, resulting in a
landslide in the area where they'd been staying. Liam and Tom had been swept away to
their deaths.

It was only a matter of weeks before this
baby was due and she had no idea how she
was going to do everything on her own.

'Kayla. Let me in.'

Oh, yes, and Jamie had suddenly turned
into a stalker, showing up all the time and
trying to convince her he was out to win
Father of the Year. It was a complete turnaround from his visits earlier in the pregnancy when he'd been more interested in
catching up with his brother than acknowl-
edging the baby. The way she'd preferred it.
Life was difficult enough for her trying to
come to terms with the fact she was about to
become a mum without having to deal with

him and those unwanted feelings he kept stirring up inside her.

'I don't care if you are the father of this baby. You're practically a stranger and I have no intention of letting you interfere in my life.' Kayla slammed the door and promptly burst into tears. This was all such a mess.

She rubbed her hand over her huge belly. 'I'm so sorry, little one. We all wanted better for you.'

He or she should have had happily married parents with a life mapped out. Not an unlovable mother and a playboy father who'd never wanted the responsibility of a baby, handing it over to those better suited to the parenting role. She'd let this child down before it had even been born. How the hell was she going to provide the upbringing it deserved? It wasn't as though she had good role models to follow. She was going into this blind.

Another veil of tears fell, soaking the delicate silk scarf around her neck; Liam had bought it for her last birthday. Her brother had known she'd adore it because of the motif. The dragonfly was her personal totem and a powerful symbol of change and light in many cultures. In this case Liam said it represented the start of their new life and the rebirth of their family.

Now it was a reminder of everything she'd lost.

She slipped the scarf off her neck and draped it around the photograph of Liam and Tom on their wedding day. Happiness radiated from their smiles as they gazed at each other, so full of hope for their future together. Only to have it so cruelly snatched away from them a short time later.

'I have as much right as you to be here.' Jamie's voice carried down the hall to interrupt her grief and cause her temper to flare again. His constant presence was preventing her from focusing on more important matters. Such as the prospect of becoming a single parent.

'How did you get in?' She watched helplessly as he stalked into the living room as though he owned the place.

He swung the house key around his finger on the hand-stitched felt key ring she'd made with Tom's name on it as a moving-in present. 'This is my house too, remember? You're not the only one who lost a brother and it's about time you stopped avoiding me. We have a lot to discuss.'

Their brothers had left everything to the two of them in their wills, making it impossible for Kayla to avoid him unless she sold up, and there was enough upheaval without having to move to a new house as well. It was a pity the wills hadn't been updated since the surrogacy arrangement. Then they might have had some idea of what it was they were expected to do.

Jamie threw himself onto the settee and she worried he was ensconced for the night. There was no other choice for her but to join him. Although it took her slightly longer to ease herself and her bump into a chair.

'I thought you'd made it abundantly clear from the start you didn't want anything to do with this baby.' She wished that were still the case. He had a choice where she didn't. No matter what happened, she had to give birth and be a mother to this baby.

'That was when I thought I was going to be nothing but a sperm donor to make my brother's dream of being a father come true. I wanted Tom to be happy. No matter how unconventional, I wanted to see his dream of having a family come true. Now he's gone this baby will need someone to look out for it.'

'I'm looking out for it. I *am* the mother.' He wasn't the only one who'd done this with the intention of making the couple happy. This wasn't the time to be searching for accolades. Jamie had provided his little swimmers because Tom's hadn't been doing the job they were supposed to, but she'd been the one who'd gone through the intrusive medically assisted insemination process.

It was she who'd carried the baby all this time. She was the one whose body would never be the same again.

'In case you've forgotten, I'm the father.'

'I haven't forgotten. I'm giving you the opportunity to walk away. As you'd planned from the start.' She didn't want to parent on her own, but it was preferable to a lifetime of being tied to this man.

Kayla had moved to London with Liam nearly fifteen years ago to escape the control of their parents and she wasn't going to tie herself to a man she hardly knew now. That hadn't ended well the last time she'd been conned into it. She'd been left broken-hearted and homeless when she'd rebelled against Paul's dominance in their relationship.

It wasn't that long since she'd lost her brother. She was vulnerable, and she wasn't going to let anyone take advantage of that.

Jamie stood up. He was imposing at his full height, which had to be a good foot taller than her five-foot-three-inch frame. Especially when he was dressed in his GP's sharp suit and tie and she was in her ever-expanding maternity leggings and voluminous, stretch jersey, dark grey bump-coverer.

He strode towards her with such purpose her mouth suddenly went dry.

Then he leaned down and whispered, 'Not going to happen.'

The ebb and flow of a shiver brought the tiny hairs on her arms to attention as his breath warmed her cheek. He gave her scant time to linger on her body's reaction and walked away again towards the kitchen.

When she managed to compose herself enough to follow him she wished she hadn't. Her sense of incredulity and temper rose further with every cupboard he opened, showing no respect for the fact this had been her home for the better part of a year. He might have inherited a share through tragic circumstances, but his lack of good manners and bold self-entitlement were not aiding their already strained relationship.

'Don't you have any proper food in this place?' He was rummaging in the fridge, turning his nose up at the contents as he inspected them.

'I only have *proper* food. It's much healthier than that processed junk you probably favour.' Liam and Tom had shared her healthy approach to food, but Jamie didn't look as though he could be sustained by lettuce and carrots alone.

'Give me a dirty, big burger any day,' he grumbled, confirming the belief he was a man who enjoyed the red-meat-fuelled lifestyle of his caveman ancestors.

Although lean, Jamie was solid muscle and sinew. She could see that by the way his tailored shirt clung to his torso, and his thighs stretched the fabric of his tight-fitting black trousers. This was someone who needed protein to fuel his workout. He'd be more inclined towards swimming rather than being a gym bunny, she decided. Mainly because she could imagine him gliding through the water with those powerful limbs, showing off that streamlined body in nothing but a tight-fitting pair of swim trunks.

'I said, we're going to have to do a grocery shop or I'll starve to death here.'

Kayla blinked away her glistening-wet, semi-naked fantasy to centre on the fully dressed version of Jamie, whose mouth was twitching as he tried not to laugh. It was then she realised she'd been staring, and it hadn't gone unnoticed. She blamed the sudden heat consuming her body on the rise of her blood pressure at having an unwanted visitor going through her things. Not due to any thoughts of Tom's big brother with his wet hair curling at the nape of his neck or water sluicing over his naked body.

'You—you don't live here. My cupboards are none of your business,' she blustered, slamming shut all the doors he'd opened during his plundering.

'Well, here's the thing, Kayla. It was one thing being the biological father only and Tom taking responsibility for raising this child. Now he's not here, the baton passes to me and I'm afraid I'm not going to sit back and let your hippy-dippy ways dictate my baby's life.' He folded his arms and rested his backside against her worktop as casual as he liked.

Meanwhile, she was sure she was about to combust into flames. His baby. Calling her hippy-dippy. He'd wiped out her credibility as a mother in one insult. She didn't think being a vegetarian and using meditation as a form of stress relief justified anyone making fun of her. It was her way of taking back her life and being at peace with herself.

Kayla opened her mouth, then closed it again before she said something very unladylike. Once the moment passed she called upon her rational self to counter his ill-judged argument.

'First of all—' her voice was louder than she'd intended so she dialled it back before he accused her of being hysterical '—this baby is not a baton. It is a human being that has been growing inside me. Therefore, I think it's safe to say you're not going to *let* me do anything. I'm its mother.'

'And I'm its father.'

The man was infuriating beyond words.

Count to ten, Kayla, and don't even think about launching that frying pan at his head, even if it is within arm's reach.

Jamie levered himself off the worktop and walked towards her. Kayla immediately backed away. She didn't enjoy confrontation. Usually, she did her best to avoid it when raised voices and tempers brought back memories of a childhood best forgotten.

Unfortunately, Jamie brought out the worst in her and vice versa. In all the time she'd known Tom he'd never shown anything but adoration for his older brother. He'd talked about him in such glowing terms Kayla had expected him to be a saint. From her perspective he was purely an annoyance.

Especially when they both knew she'd been prepared to walk out of that coffee shop and engage in some sordid afternoon shenanigans if their brothers hadn't turned up that day. She didn't like him knowing he was a weakness where she was concerned in case he used it to get the upper hand.

'Look, Kayla, I'm not here to fight with you. I just want to make sure you and the baby are healthy. This is the last link I have to Tom and the only family I have left.' It was a heartfelt plea, but there was no way she was giving him room to start dictating to her. She'd had enough of that growing up.

'So, what are you going to do? Draw up a contract and a diet plan according to what you deem a suitable lifestyle? We're not in some weird relationship where I'm happy to submit to your dominant will. I'm not that kind of girl.'

'Wow.'

'What's wrong? Have you never had a woman talk back to you before?' With his looks and his status as a partner in his GP practice, no doubt he was used to people doing his bidding with no questions asked.

The rumble as he laughed did things to her insides she wasn't prepared for. 'No. It's just interesting that's where your mind went.'

'Liam and Tom might have left you half of this house, but you have absolutely no claim on my body.' Her mind chose to interpret those words differently than they were intended. Forbidden images of Jamie's mouth and hands possessing her sprang from nowhere, causing chaos within.

This pregnancy brought more problems than heartburn and weight gain. Especially when these feelings were so rare she didn't think she'd experienced them even with her exes. A problem that had ended all her relationships and made her consider this surrogacy in the first place.

Sex wasn't something she'd been able to fully enjoy when she couldn't find it in herself to give control of her body completely to someone else. The same could be said about love.

Now a few arrogant words from a man who had a knack for getting under her skin were already wreaking havoc on her insides again.

One thing was for sure, she had to find some way to get Jamie out of her life so she and the baby could live the life Tom and Liam would now never be a part of.

'Technically, whilst you're pregnant with my child, I do have an interest in your body.' Jamie couldn't help himself. There was more than a hint of truth in those words and not solely for the baby she was carrying.

Small and curvy even before she got pregnant, Kayla physically wasn't his usual type. Her honey-blond hair fell in messy natural ringlets around her shoulders, as chaotic as her rolled-through-a-jumble-sale fashion sense. The layers of mismatched vintage clothes she favoured, most people would have consigned to the dustbin.

Personality wise there was a major clash between them, as this current exchange would attest to. She was hard work, a pain in the backside he could do without. Yet, since losing Tom and Liam, he hadn't been able to keep away from her. He knew it was more than their shared grief but hoped his sudden interest in her would end once the baby was born. Anything else would have disaster written all over it. Her shudder of obvious disgust at his comment was proof of that.

'My body is absolutely none of your business.' She folded her arms across her blossoming cleavage and Jamie tried to avert his stare.

'Ditto. So, I'll thank you to stop looking at me as though I'm a piece of meat.' By the way she'd been ogling him earlier he'd say her pregnancy hormones were running riot. It was a reminder of that day in the café when they'd come close to succumbing to temptation. Thank goodness they hadn't, when things were complicated enough between them.

'I was not!' Her reddening cheeks gave her away.

'Let's get one thing straight here, Kayla.' He flicked the kettle on and lifted a mug down from the cupboard. 'My only interest is in the baby you're carrying.'

'Mine too.' Composure regained, she walked right up to him. Close enough for him to drink in her floral scent. It was likely something she made herself from daisies and buttercups under the light of a full moon.

Kayla opened the cupboard above his head, lifted out a handmade, slightly wonky, blue-glazed earthenware mug and set it down on the counter.

'I assume you have a birth plan in place? I don't imagine the event is something either of our brothers would have left to chance.' Even if Kayla seemed the sort of person to let nature take its course. There was a very bohemian quality to her. As though she'd be more at home in some hippy commune living off the earth and communing with nature than working nine-to-five and living in a suburban semi.

'I'm having a natural birth. At home.'

He should have known.

'Not happening.'

'Excuse me? It was what your brother, Liam, and I wanted. You can't just swan in here—'

'And what? Want what's best for my baby? Which is to be born in a hospital where the best medical care is at hand should anything go wrong?'

Kayla couldn't believe what she was hearing. They had planned as peaceful a welcome into the world as they could provide. Now, Jamie was storming in demanding as much noise, disruption and upheaval that came with hospital births in comparison. No way was she having that. The days of letting anyone walk over her were long gone.

'In case you're not aware, I was a qualified midwife before I became a doula. I know the difference it can make to mum and baby when a birth is at home, surrounded by familiar faces, enveloped in love rather than machines and overworked staff. That's why I changed careers.'

It had been difficult for her to adhere to the rules laid out by the hospital management when births didn't run to their specific time-table or targets. She realised quickly after qualifying she'd much rather devote herself to one family at a time than be on a conveyor belt moving from one mother to the next without making any real personal connection.

'Then you know there are potential risks with any pregnancy. Complications during a home birth can't be dealt with as effectively as they could be at the hospital.'

'I'm qualified to make those kinds of decisions that might warrant a hospital transfer.' It didn't happen often, but in emergencies she would encourage medical intervention where it was needed. The welfare of baby and mother were always top priority.

'Tell me, are you planning on giving birth naked and alone in a field?' There was that patronising tone she'd come to know well when involved in a heated discussion with another medical professional on the subject.

'You might not agree with my methods but please don't mock them.'

'It's hard not to,' he muttered, reinforcing the idea that a calm, peaceful birth wasn't going to be possible anywhere with him around.

'What is so wrong in wanting to be in the comfort of my own home, listening to the music of my choice and letting nature take its course?' There'd been too much upset already during this pregnancy and the least she could do now was give this baby a smooth transition from the warm cocoon of her body into its new environment.

'It's selfish,' he answered without taking time to think about what it meant to anyone other than him.

'No, it's simply an alternative to a hospital birth. Women have been doing it for centuries. I think I'll manage.'

'What? You're going to deliver the baby yourself? I'm sorry, but this is crazy. I've already lost my brother. I'm not prepared to jeopardise my baby for the sake of your whim to raise a flower-child. I don't think the sixties were all they were cracked up to be, you know. There was a higher mortality rate back then, likely for this very reason.'

Breathe in. Breathe out. Don't punch things.

Kayla hadn't realised dinosaurs still roamed the earth masquerading as pretty doctors, but Jamie was living proof.

'There are such things as friends. I know that concept might not be familiar to you if this is how you speak to everyone you meet. I have my own doula to assist with labour as well as a community midwife.'

'Great. It's reassuring to know there'll be two of you howling at the moon and stinking the place out with incense.'

She didn't know where he plucked these ideas about home births from. He was a GP, for heaven's sake. She was sure he'd dealt with them in his time. This seemed more personal to her. As though he simply disapproved of her and her life choices when, really, he knew nothing about her.

All his talk so far surrounded his wishes

for his baby, relegating her to the role of incubator who shouldn't have any opinion of her own.

'I really don't care what you think, Jamie. This is my safe space. My body. My baby. My birth plan. You won't be here anyway, so it won't affect you.' At this rate the baby would be cutting its first teeth by the time she told him it had arrived.

There was no way she was having him anywhere near her, stressing her out during the most important, and unexpected, phase of her life as she transitioned into motherhood. Given the chance he'd probably be shouting instructions like her old PE teacher, calling her a slacker and pushing her until she was sure her lungs would explode. That wasn't the atmosphere she was striving for on this occasion.

'Who says I won't be here?'

'This is my first baby and I've still got a few weeks until my due date. The chances are slim you'll be in the vicinity when I go into labour.' She certainly wasn't going to tell him.

Jamie Garrett hovering over her every decision was the last thing on her wish list. It was the worst possible scenario after losing the men she'd thought were raising this child.

'I'm going to increase those odds.'

'How?' She was compelled to ask, though she did so with a sigh. He was exhausting and as soon as she got shot of him she'd do a bit of meditation to clear her chakras from the negativity he left in his wake. She might even listen to the CD of whale music the boys had given her as a joke present. It would be her way of sticking two fingers up at the biological father-to-be who'd be horrified at the very idea.

'I'm moving in.' The self-satisfied smirk strengthened the impact of the bombshell.

She'd been wrong. This was the worst possible scenario and she was powerless to do anything about it.

CHAPTER THREE

'THIS ISN'T HOW it was supposed to be. Liam and Tom were going to be the parents. Once I gave birth, my part was done. It certainly wasn't intended to be a dictatorship run by you.' Kayla promptly burst into tears and Jamie's elation at getting the upper hand instantly gave way to something more sympathetic.

He hadn't come here to antagonise her. Since Tom's death, all he'd wanted was to be part of his baby's life and to be a dad. The flirty nature of their relationship had to change in the wake of their loss. He'd changed, knowing he had new responsibilities to meet, and Kayla was a part of that new chapter. Upsetting her further wasn't going to do anyone any good.

'Why don't you sit down?' He pulled over

one of the high-back stools from the breakfast bar. Now that pig-headedness had left her he could see how vulnerable she was. It must be hard for that little body of hers to be carrying that bump along with the hopes and dreams of both their brothers.

'Stop telling me what to do!' she yelled at him, her face scarlet as she vented her fury. Tears soon followed the outburst as her sobs ricocheted around the kitchen walls before hitting Jamie square in the chest. So much for wanting the best for mother and baby. He'd added more stress on top of already losing her brother.

Jamie backed away, crouched down with his hands raised in surrender as though pacifying a dangerous animal before it could attack. 'I was only trying to make you more comfortable. I don't want the baby to be in any danger because you're all worked up.'

He didn't suppose she had a blood-pressure cuff tucked away with her bongo drums and crystals in her birthing accessories. In this instance he might well make a dash out to his car where he had one in his bag for emergencies. He'd like to check her blood pressure. That was if she'd consent to him being close without hitting him with something.

'Shut up. Shut up. Shut up!' Her voice gradually grew louder until she was verging on the edge of hysteria. Kayla stomped her foot on the floor with that final instruction.

Jamie could only watch in horror as a trickle of liquid soaked her trousers and splashed on the tiled floor.

'Okay. Don't panic, but I think your waters have just broken.' He dared to venture into her personal space, put an arm around her shoulders and guided her towards the living room.

'It's too early.' She was clearly in shock since she permitted him to lead her.

'Not really. The baby's viable at this stage. No need to panic. Now, do you have something I can put down to protect the sofa?'

She was waddling even more than usual, but she didn't put up any further protest. 'There are towels in the wooden chest in the corner.' There was a dazed quality to her voice he wasn't sure was preferable to the ranting she'd been doing only moments earlier.

The area she directed him to was separate from the rest of the furnishings in the room. A circle of primary-coloured over-sized cushions on the floor had been carefully arranged. It had the appearance of a giant, gaudy bird nest, but this wasn't the time for him to make any further mocking comments. He ignored the questions burning to be asked, the jokes begging to be made, to retrieve a couple of faded grey towels from the chest.

'I'll phone ahead to the labour ward and let them know you're coming in. My car's outside. I can drive you to hospital.' He covered the seat cushions as best he could to enable her to sit down until he brought the car around to the front door.

'How many times do I have to tell you I want a home birth? Cherry is my doula. Phone her and my midwife. Their numbers are in the birth plan in my bag.' She directed him back to the weird cushion nest where her labour bag was sitting waiting for this very moment.

'I'll phone them for you but as you're not full term I'd prefer to get you to hospital.' He was doing his best not to be confrontational but when they held such conflicting views on the subject he knew he was fighting a losing battle.

'This is your fault. You've ruined everything. I'm not letting you take this away from me too.' Kayla let out an anguished cry and doubled over, clutching her belly.

'Contraction?' He crouched down in front of her, timing it with his watch.

She nodded, her face contorted with pain, and Jamie wished he could swap places with her. All he could do was hold her hand and wait until the pain subsided. He didn't care that she'd almost cut off his circulation she was squeezing him so hard.

It was his fault. He'd been so determined to be part of this he'd trodden all over Kayla's feelings to the point of starting her labour. When all she'd wanted was a peaceful birth.

'I'll phone Cherry, so she can come and sit with you, and I'll let the midwife know labour's started.' It was the least he could do.

'You'll stay with me until she comes, right?'

He made a move to get the numbers from the file, only for Kayla to grab his hand again. It was the first indication that she wanted his help, though he knew it was only through her fear of the unknown. He wanted to be here for her, holding her and providing the support he'd so far failed to give her.

'If it's all right with you I'll be staying until the baby's born.' That way he could make his own observations and decisions about how the labour was progressing. If he had any inkling at all anything was wrong, he'd be straight on the phone to the hospital.

'I don't want you interfering any more than you already have, Jamie. Get Cherry here.'

'How about a compromise? I'll stay, at a distance, but the first sign of anything untoward and we're back to civilisation for help.'

'Fine. Just get Cherry.' Another sob erupted, followed by a further contraction. This baby was apparently in a hurry to meet its parents.

Kayla tried her best to think away the pain, to focus on the beautiful baby she would have at the end of this. To no avail. She'd been through innumerable labours and births, but panic had set in when she'd experienced that first vice-like pain for herself. She wasn't ready to become a mother.

'I'm surprised none of my patients ever slapped me when I told them to breathe through this. It's easier said than done.' With the next wave of agony, she attempted to channel it into Jamie via his fingers. He deserved to share in every aspect of this labour if he was so keen.

'I guess you don't want me telling you you're a good girl, then?' His grin soon changed to a grimace as she tightened her grip. She trusted there was sufficient venom in her stare to prevent him from making further patronising comments even in jest.

The sound of the doorbell saved his fingers from being completely mangled but did leave her temporarily without an outlet for her pain. It was worse being alone for the few seconds it took him to answer the door. That brief time, sitting on her own in the quiet room with her baby on the way, confronted her with the truth she had to do this without Liam and Tom's support. Heaven help her, she needed someone with her for this. Even if it had to be Jamie.

'Hey, honey. Is it that time already?' A waft of gardenias announced Cherry's arrival and was enough to set off a new rainfall down Kayla's face.

'Contractions are already four minutes apart. The midwife is on her way.' It was Jamie who provided the details Cherry needed to help organise the labour. Strange, when he'd made it clear he didn't agree with her methods, but he was here, supporting her decisions after all.

Cherry came to sit beside her on the couch. 'Goodness. We'd better get you organised. Jamie—'

'Dr Garrett,' he corrected her. It was likely his attempt to assert some authority in a situation where he knew he had none.

Cherry, like Kayla, wasn't someone easily intimidated. 'I'm sure Kayla has told you we want to create an informal atmosphere here. If you don't mind, I'll stick to Jamie. Now, if you could go and make us all a cup of tea, I'll help Kayla change out of these wet clothes.'

Everything in his tense jaw said he did mind. Nevertheless, he did leave the room for them to have their privacy.

'The father, I take it?' Her best friend, doula, and all-round good egg, Cherry, helped her to strip off.

'Not the one I'd planned on having around but he's insisting on it.'

'That's not a bad thing when you don't have Liam and Tom around any more. I mean, Debbie and I are here for you, but, you know, he's family.' Between them they managed to re-dress Kyla in the cotton nightdress she'd left by her pregnancy pad for labour. Although, if she felt the desire to do this naked at a later stage she'd still be shedding her outward skin, regardless if Jamie was here or not. Giving birth was not a time to worry about inhibitions.

'You and Debbie are more family than Jamie. I hardly know him.'

'Give him a chance, Kay. You two are in this together. Besides, he's kinda hot. I'm surprised you two didn't just conceive the old-fashioned way. I'm sure it would've been a hell of a lot more fun.'

'Cherry!' She didn't share the fact it had nearly happened because any attraction had been rendered irrelevant. It was clear they couldn't be in a room together without rowing. Sharing a bed would've caused fireworks. That was probably why she couldn't get the idea out of her head.

'What? I can still enjoy looking at a pretty package even if it's not quite to my taste.'

'I think your wife might have something to say about that.' Her best friends were happily married but Kayla still experienced an irrational possessiveness over a man who wasn't hers and never likely to be.

'Debbie would be on my side.'

'He's the total opposite to his brother. Jamie is rude, annoying…rude, and a dinosaur.'

'At least one of those statements is false. Would a dinosaur father a baby for his gay brother and his husband? I think not.'

Ugh. She was being too logical at a time Kayla was well within her rights to detest the father of her baby. She'd seen her share of women cursing the men who'd made them go through the pain of childbirth and she was no exception. Even if it was for a different reason. He wasn't Liam or Tom.

'Whose side are you on anyway? I thought a doula was supposed to keep me calm and agree with whatever I say?'

'Not quite.'

'Aagh!' That intrusive cramping squeezed her body tight and stole away any thoughts on anything other than the pain.

'That's it. Deep breaths. In and out. Remember this is all for a reason. Your body is doing the most important job in the world for you and getting ready to deliver this baby.'

Kayla closed her eyes and visualised the tiny wonder she was going through all of this for and the joy she should feel at finally holding it in her arms. Not the terror that had her in its grip at the thought of what the future held for them both. She held Cherry's hand until the contraction eased.

'Sorry, Kay. From now on I'll have my

doula hat on and forget dishing out advice as your sassy best friend.'

'Don't let her disappear altogether. Your kind of truth is exactly why I wanted you with me for this.' Tears began to well again at all the plans she'd made with the proud fathers-to-be.

Tom and Liam had been just as excited as her about the prospect of the birth and having Cherry there too had seemed like the icing on the cake. One big happy family. Now Cherry was the only thing left from those plans.

'Tea's ready, or whatever passes for tea in this house.' Jamie returned, eyeing the cups on the tray with some suspicion. No doubt he'd prefer strong builder's tea full of caffeine, milk and sugar to her herbal alternatives. Too bad.

'There's no room for your negativity here, Jamie. This birth is going to be a positive experience and that extends to accepting how I take my tea.' She helped herself to a raspberry tea and waited to see how he'd react to his.

'That's right, and you need to rest between

these contractions, Kayla. Sip some of your tea and close your eyes for a while. You'll need all your strength.' Cherry plumped the cushions around her back and Kayla did as suggested.

Experience watching her own patients told her labour could be a long and difficult road. The reward was always worth it in the end, but it took a toll on the mothers all the same. The unpredictable nature of labour meant any breaks should be taken advantage of when possible.

Another contraction hit and stole away any idea of relaxation. They seemed to be coming thick and fast and she couldn't believe she'd worried that everyone would be sitting around the house waiting for labour to start. It was well and truly under way.

She could see Jamie frowning behind Cherry. 'They're only three minutes apart now. Where is this midwife?'

'She probably thought she had a little more time to get here since it's Kayla's first baby. I'm sure she's on her way.' Cherry's calm response prevented Kayla from panicking more than she already was. It was natural to be afraid of the impending birth, but she didn't need the extra stress of doing it without her midwife.

'So is the baby.' His tone was accusatory, and, she suspected, directed at her.

'I'll give her another ring. Jamie, could you sit here with Kayla until I get back?' Neither protested at Cherry's request. He simply came to her side where he needed to be.

'Are you comfortable?'

'What do you think?' She'd never been more uncomfortable in her whole life.

He ignored her death stare and her barking response. 'I mean, can I help you get into a better position?'

Okay, maybe he wasn't a complete nuisance. He could have his uses.

'My back is killing me. I don't know how women do this for hours, sometimes days on end. I want it over already.'

'At this rate you might just have your wish. Why don't we try you leaning over this and see if we can find you some relief?' He pulled over the maroon velvet ottoman she kept her knitting in. Kayla noted he was using 'we' now. He'd committed to this birth with her and to be honest she was glad. She had a friend and support in Cherry, but if the midwife didn't get here, she might need his medical expertise. He wouldn't let harm come to this baby that had become so precious to him and therefore had to take care of her too until it arrived.

The pressure was already starting to build again, and she wanted to sob. Regardless that this was a happy event, she was tired and in pain already. She needed her big brother to hold her hand and tell her everything was going to be all right, the way he'd done her entire life.

Jamie helped heave her up from her position on the floor until she was on her knees, forearms resting on top of the ottoman. 'We're going to time this one.'

Kayla rocked her body, attempting to relieve the pain, resting her weight on her arms. The firm pressure at the base of her spine helped ease it and she realised it was Jamie, rubbing her back without her having to ask.

This one lasted longer than the others. Kayla heard a low moaning in the distance before she realised it was coming from deep inside her gut. She felt, and sounded, like a heifer about to give birth to its calf.

'That's it, Kayla. This one's nearly over.' The reassurance was as far from patronising as Jamie could get. He was encouraging her, cheering her on and telling her she could do this when she was full of doubt.

When there was a pause, he helped her back into a sitting position. She closed her eyes and waited for sleep. Jamie's hand brushed the damp strands of her hair away from her brow. The cool touch of his skin against hers was a relief in itself and she held his hand there for maximum effect.

'You like that, huh?'

She didn't have to open her eyes to know he was smirking, knowing that he'd been needed here after all.

'Uh-huh.'

'I'll get you a cold compress when Cherry comes back.'

On cue, she heard her say her goodbyes

over the phone as she walked into the room. 'Kayla—'

At the sound of uncertainty in the usually unflappable Cherry, Kayla snapped her eyes open, immediately on her guard.

Cherry approached from the opposite side to Jamie and patted her shoulder. 'I don't want you to worry, but the midwife's been in an accident on the way over. She's fine but she's going to be a while longer.'

Concentrate on the breathing. One, two, three...

Jamie dropped her hand and got to his feet. She watched him pace the room with growing unease, rubbing his temple and doing his best not to explode at her.

Four, five, six...

'What happens now?'

'She's phoned an ambulance for you and explained what's happened. It all depends how quickly they can get here.' That deathly pale colour didn't suit Cherry at all. It wasn't her fault this had happened any more than it was Kayla's. No one could have predicted this. Except for Jamie.

'I could still drive you there. If that's what you want?' The pleading was there in his eyes for her to go with him. To make some effort to get help in case something went wrong with the birth. She understood why, but his peace of mind wasn't going to come before hers.

'No. I'm having my baby at home.' She kept her voice as calm and measured as she could, to let him know she was making this decision with a clear head. Despite having no pain relief or a midwife, she was still going to do this her way.

Instead of arguing with her, he turned to Cherry. 'Have you delivered a baby before?'

'No, I've seen plenty but it's not my job to get in the way of midwives or doctors doing theirs.'

'Doulas are there to support the mums, not intervene in any medical procedures. Generally, they're not qualified for that.' Kayla was but only because she'd worked as a midwife beforehand.

'I want to make sure we know what we're taking on here if the ambulance doesn't arrive before the baby does.' Unlike Jamie, Kayla didn't want to think about that, but it was a scenario they had to consider.

'All signs have pointed towards a healthy baby thus far. There's no reason why this shouldn't be a straightforward birth without complications.' If there had been any problems during the pregnancy she would've been the first to put herself in the hands of the doctors. Her wishes wouldn't come at any cost.

'Let's hope so.' His sarcastic, 'It's only life or death,' follow-up comment hung unsaid in the air between them.

'What about you, Jamie? Have you ever delivered a baby?' Thank goodness Cherry was here to provide a buffer between them and some common sense. In case any of them had forgotten in the heat of the moment, he was a qualified doctor.

'A long time ago and it was an emergency. No one's choice. Especially mine.' He could continue to argue if he wished but this was still happening. Her belly began to tighten, her body gearing up for another round of fun.

'You're a doctor, I'm a midwife. I'm sure

we'll…manage.' She ended on a gasp, her breath stolen by the strength of the contraction.

'Good. This surge is powerful. It's a sign we're getting close.' It was the kind of positive language she used as a doula too, but not even Cherry's well-intentioned words could stop the sobs accompanying the now relentless stage of the birthing process.

She clung onto the fingers wrapped around hers but was dismayed to find they were Cherry's, not Jamie's. He was on his way out of the door, making her heart sink into the soles of her bare feet. If he left her now there was no chance they would ever work together as parents to this baby. Co-parenting required commitment and respect. Not stamping of feet until they got their own way. That went for her too. She might not have been ecstatic about his involvement, but he had earned his place here. If he still wanted it.

That dull ache at the base of her spine was becoming unbearable now. The groan she emitted was cathartic, but it was only when

Cherry helped her into a position on all fours she found any relief.

'Where did Jamie go? I need him.' Everything around her shifted out of focus as she entered some sort of trance state, giving herself over to mother nature.

Her fevered forehead cooled with the application of a wet flannel placed against her burning skin.

'I thought you'd gone,' she managed, in between deep breaths, and hoped she wasn't hallucinating Jamie's return to her side.

He furrowed his forehead into a frown. 'You want to give birth here so here is where I'll be.'

He seemed irritated she would think anything less of him, but he'd surprised her by compromising for her benefit so soon. She'd feel safer knowing he was on hand to help if no one else got here on time. Not that she had much time to dwell on anything but herself for very long.

'I can't do this any more,' she wept, wanting to collapse into a deep sleep and wake up when it was all over. Better still, to wake up and find the whole surrogacy idea had been a dream.

'You can't go back now. Don't worry, it won't be long.' He was saying and doing all the right things. It made a change from their constant battle to be top dog. Jamie was all right when he wasn't trying to take over all the time.

'Let's get her back against the cushions.' He even did as Cherry bade him and helped manoeuvre her when there was a reprieve from the contractions.

'I'll take this away again. I don't think it's helping much now.' He removed the not so cold flannel and rested his palm on her forehead instead.

'That's nice. You're nice.' The slight pressure along with his cool touch was equally welcome.

He brushed her hair away from her face again and repeated the soothing action until he'd nearly convinced her sleep was possible. Her body wasn't long in reminding her that it wasn't.

A strong pulling sensation tugged between

her legs, along with the urge to get into a squatting position. 'Give me a hand to get up, please.'

'Do you want to push?' Jamie moved front and centre, getting ready to deliver this baby who didn't seem to care who was, or wasn't, present for the arrival.

'Kayla doesn't want to traumatise the baby by forcing it out. The birth is to happen naturally.' Cherry was only repeating what her client had told her, but on this occasion, Jamie was right. Her body was telling her to push.

'I think it's happening whether I like it or not.'

'On the next contraction I want you to bear down. I'm going to have to push your nightdress up out of the way, okay?'

It wasn't as though she could give birth without him seeing her, so she nodded. He was a doctor and it seemed ridiculous for her to start feeling shy now. Then the pain reminded her she didn't care about anything other than getting this over with.

'We can get through this.' The other member of the cheer squad continued to rub her back, showing her support whatever decision Kayla made.

Both shouted their encouragement as she entered the final stage of her labour quicker than anyone had anticipated.

'Hold on to my shoulders and hurt me as much as you need to.' He made her smile with the sincere offer.

'I'll hold you to that.'

'It's a one-time deal. Only to be redeemed during labour,' he said with a smile, which disappeared with her own as she cried out again.

'Where is that ambulance?' He rolled up his shirt sleeves as she pushed down on his broad shoulders, using him as leverage to encourage the baby out. In any other circumstances a father delivering his own baby should've been a wonderful bonding experience, but this wasn't a normal set-up. With Jamie here, it made her feel less alone in her unexpected induction into parenthood.

'Close your eyes and see your baby emerging into this new world.' Cherry's voice was the calm in the storm, keeping her grounded when she wanted to scream.

'The baby's crowning. I can see the head. You're doing great, Kayla. Our baby's nearly here.'

Our baby. That nugget barely registered amid her fugue, but it was an important reminder all the same. This was Jamie's child too. No matter how unconventional the conception.

There was such a buzz in the room as they anticipated the moment they were all here for, Kayla dug deep for another burst of energy to push through the pain.

'Kayla, I need you to hold off on pushing for a while. Cherry, can you come and give me a hand?'

'Jamie? What's wrong?' She struggled to sit up. The atmosphere changed as Cherry and Jamie exchanged concerned glances. It was a surge of nausea that rose in her this time through fear she'd made a mistake by having the baby at home after all.

'The umbilical cord is caught around the

baby's neck. I just need you to slow this down until I can untangle it.'

She'd probably seen and dealt with more occurrences of this than Jamie but that didn't stop her from visualising her baby suffocating.

'Panting breaths now, Kayla. There's no need to panic. Jamie's got this.'

The short, panting breaths Cherry coached her through helped stave off that urge to push, giving Jamie time to work so baby's oxygen supply wasn't cut off to the brain. This was his baby too and he wouldn't let anything happen to it when he'd fought so hard to be here with her.

'That's it, Kayla. The cord's free now. When the next contraction comes, baby will be here.' It was the pride with which Jamie delivered the news that gave her the confidence that everything was going to be all right after all.

Jamie couldn't quite believe he was here doing this. Delivering his own baby. None of this was what he'd expected to happen when he'd signed on to help his brother have a baby with his husband. Yet he wouldn't want to be anywhere other than here right now, helping Kayla as she gave birth to their son.

'It's a boy.' His cry echoed hers as he caught the slippery bundle in his hands and all the emotion surrounding the moment and the lead up to it came pouring out. He'd lost his brother, but Tom had left Jamie with this precious gift.

'Is he okay?' The panic in Kayla's voice was understandable. His blood had frozen in his veins when he'd seen that cord threatening the life of this baby before it had even begun.

He passed the baby to Cherry, so she could hand him to his mother for that all-important skin-to-skin contact.

'He's beautiful. Congratulations, Mummy and Daddy.'

Jamie was exhausted and all he'd done was catch this determined mite. It was Kayla who'd done all the hard work. Yet her eyes were bright against her flushed pink skin as she murmured a loving hello to her firstborn. He'd never seen anything so beautiful.

'You did a fantastic job, Kayla.' The gentle kiss he placed on her cheek seemed only natural as he leaned across to coo over the baby with her.

'You too,' she said, giving him a shy smile before quickly looking away again.

Hopefully this was the beginning of the thaw between them that was needed so they could move forward as parents.

The repeated thumping on the door broke through the intimate family portrait as the outside begged to be let in.

'That could be the paramedics. I'll get it.' Cherry went to open the door and left them alone with their baby for the first time.

'I think he's got your lungs,' Jamie teased as baby Garrett voiced his displeasure at great volume.

'Hmm, well, he's definitely got his daddy's temper.' She teased him right back, comparing him to the red-faced, bawling tot cradled in her arms.

He didn't care when the casual use of the

D word had hit him harder than her intended insult. Jamie was a daddy, now and for the rest of his life. Parenting was something he swore he'd never do again. It was a privileged position he had now only because his brother had lost his life.

His desire to live the rest of his life without responsibility for another life was no longer an option. The question now was to what extent he'd continue to play a part in his son's upbringing.

CHAPTER FOUR

'DAD, WOULD YOU like to cut the cord?'

It was one thing being a stand-in parent for his little brother, or a biological father who'd been ready to walk away from any responsibility. To hear someone give him that title and make him face the reality of deciding to raise this child was a whole new ball game. Jamie didn't know the first thing about looking after a baby other than what he'd read in medical books. He looked to Kayla for guidance before he answered the paramedic. It was down to her to make that call.

'I think you've earned that right, don't you?' She was glowing with happiness as she swaddled the baby in the colourful crocheted blanket he'd seen in the wooden chest along with the towels. He wasn't sure he had earned the right. Where Kayla looked natural as a mother, doubts and uncertainty suddenly clouded his judgement about his new position as a parent. With the playboy reputation Kayla had awarded him because of his inability to commit, he wasn't sure he'd make a good role model.

The judgement on his character did seem a little unfair. From the outside it might appear as though he was a love 'em and leave 'em kind of guy. However, his attitude towards relationships wasn't entirely as heartless as it might appear. He and Tom had suffered because of their parents' obvious mistake in having children. Their father had been selfish and not a man who should ever have considered having a family. It hadn't changed him. He hadn't suddenly stopped being an adrenaline junkie who preferred his own company in the outdoors because he had two young boys at home. Jamie had always been afraid of inheriting that selfish attitude and blighting some other youngster's childhood.

Oh, he'd raised Tom as best he could, but he was his brother and he'd had no choice. There was nothing to say he'd make a good father.

Especially when his behaviour since Tom had moved out hadn't been conducive to family life. He wasn't as naïve as to think a child could suddenly change him from a carefree bachelor into a doting dad. It wasn't as though he'd been contemplating settling down into family life with a significant other. This was purely down to tragic circumstances beyond his control.

Although, he was thankful he'd been here during the birth for all manner of reasons. Not only because he'd provided the medical support at a time of potential danger but because it might have changed Kayla's opinion about him. He wanted her to see him as someone she could go on this journey with, not merely as an obstacle in her path. If he was going to do this, he would need her help to guide him on the journey.

'I'm so glad you guys turned up,' he joked with the male paramedic who passed him the scissors, entrusting him to cut the cord between mother and baby. Now he was out in the world it was down to Jamie and Kayla to protect him. A thought that did nothing to quell those rising fears about his suitability as a father to this child.

'Looks as though you did pretty well without us.' There was a slap on the back to accompany the compliment, but it was Kayla, not Jamie, who was the real star. She'd stuck to her guns and because of her tenacity neither she nor the baby were experiencing any after-effects from the pain relief routinely offered in hospital. He couldn't say he could have held out so long without begging for drugs to alleviate the obvious pain of childbirth.

The high-stakes delivery had made him sweat enough to need a shower, though he'd kept his worry from Kayla. She'd needed him to be strong and confident about what he was doing, even if it hadn't been the whole truth at the time. Panicking her could have jeopardised the baby's life when his oxygen had already been restricted. He knew how differently things could've turned out if he hadn't been able to untangle that cord.

'We're just going to give mother and son a check-over before we go.' The paramedic gave him a heads-up that they needed some space to work but Jamie was only too glad to hand over the duty of care to someone else.

'Sure. I think I'll step outside for some air while you're doing that.' Jamie left them to do their checks and walked out through the front door, which was still lying open.

Kayla had Cherry with her for moral support, so he hoped she wouldn't notice his absence. Up until everything had gone pear-shaped she might have welcomed it. He'd rather not have had to step in and take the place of her midwife, but he hoped it would change her mind about the kind of man she thought he was.

He set foot onto the pavement out front and the cool air woke him up to reality. A stumble over his own feet sent him reaching for support. He backed up against the wall, the world spinning around him.

He slid down until his backside was resting on the ground, his legs flat out before him. Some of that gas and air Kayla had been keen to do without would be the ticket for him right about now. It was easy to see why men were eager for a stiff drink after their baby was born. Especially if they'd had to deliver it themselves.

A few deep breaths later and the fear of passing out began to leave him. It wasn't so much the actual birth that had taken a toll but the emotional impact of the situation. He was a dad. He had a son. Kayla was going to be okay. There were so many good things to celebrate, yet everything was tinged with sadness that Tom and Liam weren't here to be part of it.

Jamie didn't realise he'd been crying until the tears dripped off the end of his chin and splashed onto the ground.

'He's perfect.' Kayla couldn't stop staring at her son. For the first time in her life she felt as though she'd really accomplished something. She'd made this perfect little human being. Not on her own, of course—Jamie had played a vital part both before, and during, the birth. There was a lot to thank him for. He'd provided excellent medical backup when she'd needed it and been a great accompaniment to Cherry with moral support. He was obviously more than a pretty face and a smart mouth after all.

At this moment, the baby was her whole world. He was her only family and the last link she had to Liam. She only wished he could have been here to meet him.

'Is it too early to discuss a name yet?' Cherry helped the baby to latch on for that first important breastfeed to give him the best start in life.

'I think I'll talk to Jamie first.' It was the least she could do to involve him in that decision, even if she would claim the final say on the matter. Naming the child was the first of the big decisions she'd have to make. Something he'd have to live with for ever. It wasn't a responsibility she took lightly when everything she did as a parent now could have repercussions later. Her parents' every action had impacted negatively on her and she didn't want the same for him.

Tom and Liam had agreed on waiting until the baby was born to name him.

'Until we see what he looks like,' Liam had

insisted. They hadn't even wanted to know the sex beforehand, wishing to be *surprised*.

Now there was a part of her that wished they had been able to enjoy the excitement of knowing they'd have a son. If they had chosen a name she would have been able to honour those wishes now. As it was she didn't even know what surname he should have.

Although they'd joined their surnames when they'd married, O'Connell-Garrett might be too much of a mouthful to inflict on a child. There was also a fear that by giving him Jamie's surname he'd think he had more rights now than being simply the sperm donor. It was a minefield.

'We're going to head off now. You're both doing great but, remember, any problems at all and get down to the hospital.' The paramedics packed up their gear and, though she'd declined their suggestion of a check-up at the hospital, Kayla was glad they'd been here to deliver the placenta and give the baby the all-clear.

'Thank you so much for coming out. You'll excuse me if I don't see you to the door.' She was a little tender and her legs were wobbly, making walking anywhere a chore she wasn't ready to undertake yet. For tonight she expected to set up camp in her pillow fort.

'We'll probably see you again in a few years' time.'

It took a moment for her to get the joke but the thought of going through this a second time was the last thing on her mind.

'No chance.' She hadn't intended this to happen first time around. At least, not with her as the primary parent.

'That's what they all say.' The female paramedic all but pushed her jovial colleague out of the door and rolled her eyes in apology at Kayla.

With the outsiders gone, and only Cherry and the new arrival keeping her company, the house was slowly getting back to feeling like home. Even if there was a new, demanding male who was going to monopolise her time and thoughts for the rest of her life.

'Where's Jamie?' Surely, he hadn't run out on them already? He'd been an integral part of the birth and she expected him to be here.

She needed someone who understood the loss she'd suffered and the mixed emotions she was experiencing now their baby was here. Jamie was the only one who could relate, and she was desperate to know if he was feeling the same confusion and fear about suddenly becoming a parent.

'I'm sure he'll be back. Now, I'm not confident baby's getting anything. We might need to shift position a bit.' As Cherry plumped the cushions around her and tried to find a better position, the baby stopped sucking and let out a yell, clearly displeased he wasn't getting enough milk. His face was screwed up into a red ball of fury. His shrill wails tugged at the very core of her brand-new mothering instinct and she immediately wanted to pacify him. He was in such a temper his gummy mouth was too busy bawling to attempt a second time.

'Who's making all that noise in here?' The sight of Jamie walking in lifted her heart and her spirits.

'I can't get him to latch on properly.' The smallest act she couldn't do for her child somehow felt like a failure. What if she couldn't do this any better than her own mother and father and screwed his life up too as a result? The guilt would suffocate her if she thought she'd inflict the same pain on another human being as her parents had done to her and Liam both physically and mentally.

'You know yourself it can take time. Don't worry, Kayla. He's not going to starve.' When she was doing Cherry's job she told mothers the same thing, but it was such a blow not to be able to mother him properly straight away. Breastfeeding was a natural thing and it shouldn't have been a problem for her. Not when she coached other women on how to do it successfully.

'Tell him that.' No amount of cooing or cradling would settle him. Every cry was a dagger in her womb.

'May I?' Jamie stepped over to take the baby whilst she covered herself up again.

'Go for it.' He couldn't do a worse job as a father than she was currently doing as a mother.

He very gently reached out to take the

screaming infant and tucked him into the crook of his arm. It was then Kayla saw the telltale red-rimmed eyes. He'd been crying. Perhaps he'd just realised what he'd got himself into as well. Although, it was a shock to discover there was anything serious going on beyond his sarcasm and the constant teasing. She hadn't even seen him cry at the memorial service for their brothers when she'd hardly been able to stand, she'd been so overcome with the loss and grief.

Jamie had taken care of planning that day, greeted the mourners and organised the caterers as though on autopilot. She'd doubted he could've loved his brother as much as she'd loved hers when he'd been able to carry on as though his life hadn't just crumbled around him.

Seeing him now, she wondered if he hadn't simply been strong for her sake. He'd gone outside to cry tonight where she couldn't see him. She'd never know if the tears had been through pride, grief or relief at the circumstances in which their son had entered the world. It was a sign there were layers to Jamie beyond the cocky façade. Unless he was simply feeling sorry for himself, having realised exactly what he'd committed himself to.

'You have to give your mummy a break. It's been a long day, and this is all new to us.'

If there was anything more adorable than a big man cooing at a tiny baby in his arms, she'd yet to see it.

As if he were stunned by the phenomenon himself, the young master's yells subsided to a whine. Typical. He was going to be a daddy's boy to a man whose obligation was supposed to have ended when he'd deposited his seed into a plastic cup.

All the raving Tom had done about his brother raising him might have been justified. If Jamie was a natural father, what did that make her? Where did it leave her? Perhaps there were things she could learn from him after all.

'Is there anything you'd like me to help you with, Kayla?' Cherry peered at her with concerned eyes.

If Jamie hadn't been here she might have broken down and admitted her fears about not being able to breastfeed. Since he seemed to have mastered his part already, she was reluctant to do so. She was the one with the hands-on experience with babies. Now she was worried all that practical knowledge and learning meant nothing when she hadn't had a great parenting role model from the start. It wasn't in her genes.

'I might need some help getting settled for the night.' Post-birth doulas were often used as practical support as well as a shoulder to cry on when needed but things such as house-keeping no longer seemed important in the wider picture.

'What about sleeping arrangements?'

'I...um... I—we haven't discussed that. Jamie had just arrived when I went into labour.' Since his concern had been centred around the labour and subsequent birth, the subject of his moving in hadn't risen again.

Jamie stifled a laugh. 'I think Cherry was talking about you and the baby.'

'Oh.' She was sure she'd turned the same colour as her frustrated, hungry baby.

Jamie made her flush further by adding,

'Yes. It's way too early to think about that yet,' with a wink.

Teasing a delirious, exhausted new mum wasn't something she was a fan of and so she didn't respond to him directly. 'Cherry, if you could give me a hand upstairs I think I'd like to sleep in my own bed. I'll keep the baby in with me for the night.'

She didn't have a partner to worry that co-sleeping would interfere in their relationship as some couples found.

'We could run you a nice bath first if Jamie doesn't mind babysitting?'

'Not at all. You deserve a relaxing soak.' The proud daddy continued pacing the living room, rocking his son in his arms as though he'd been born to do it.

Meanwhile, Kayla didn't believe she deserved anything more than an 'I told you so' after her plans for a peaceful home birth had nearly gone so disastrously wrong.

'Are you sure? He might need a nappy change.' That first one was always a sticky, dirty job and her wicked side wanted to leave him on his own to cope with it and expose a weakness. They'd been parents for five minutes and already she'd made it into a competition. One he was winning by a mile.

'I can manage. Go.' He shooed them away and got to work setting out the changing mat and terry-towelling nappies she had waiting to be christened. She didn't even mind missing this first milestone at home if it meant there was something less for her to fail at.

Kayla stepped gingerly into the bath, closed her eyes and slid down under the bubbles. Bliss.

'Do you think I can stay here until he starts university?'

'You might be a tad wrinkly by then.' Cherry passed her a flannel and busied herself organising some old towels for her to dry off with when she did eventually get out.

'I don't think anyone would notice.' She threw the flannel over her face and blocked out the world.

'What gives, Kay? You were so happy when I put that baby in your arms. Now you're acting as though you don't want him anywhere near you. This is me speaking as your friend who wants to help, not your doula.'

It was ridiculous to be jealous of Jamie, but he was unfazed by this life-changing event when she was just so overwhelmed and underwhelming when it came to actual parenting.

'Jamie is so much better at this.' She pouted beneath her cotton face mask.

'Based on what? That the baby stopped crying when he saw him for the first time? Damn, that man could stop traffic. I don't blame him.'

Kayla snatched the flannel away to give Cherry the full effect of her death stare. 'You're not helping.'

'It's natural to be tired and emotional. Giving birth is a big deal. As for the feeding, you have to persevere. You know all this.' Cherry soaped her hair with shampoo, the gentle massage as she rinsed reminding Kayla of Jamie's tending during labour.

'At the minute it seems impossible.'

'We'll get you settled into bed, then I'll bring the baby up and you can try again.'

The bath had helped her to relax but when Cherry helped her into bed all Kayla wanted to do was sleep. The renewed cries from downstairs reminded her that was going to be a thing of the past.

In the end Cherry didn't have to go anywhere. Jamie knocked on the bedroom door, the baby's increasing frustration over his mother's failure to feed him sufficiently echoing through the house.

'Come in.' She propped herself up on the pillows and hoped she looked more presentable in a clean nightshirt than when he'd last seen her.

'Hey. Sorry, but I think he's looking to be fed again.' With an apology, Jamie stepped into her bedroom and handed the baby over.

It seemed absurd in the circumstances that this should be the first time he'd set foot in here when they'd conceived this child together. However, if he was the only capable parent around here she might ask him to stick around for a while longer.

The baby grizzled against her, sending her anxiety levels into the roof.

'I'll leave you to it.' Jamie backed out of the room and it was on the tip of her tongue to ask him to stay. Even though he couldn't help her with this, his presence kept her grounded. He was the closest thing around she had to family now. Apart from this baby they'd created between them.

'Okay, let's see if we can get this little one sorted out.' With some assistance, Cherry got them into a nursing position. His hungry mouth latched onto Kayla and she gasped at the first sharp pain. Any discomfort she experienced soon faded into insignificance when he began to feed in earnest.

'He's doing it!' She watched his angry face even out into contentment as he suckled.

'You did it.' Cherry's praise wasn't necessary to make her feel as though she'd achieved something, but it was nice to have someone witness and acknowledge the progress. Doing this one thing right helped her believe that there was a possibility of being a better parent than the ones she'd been born to.

'Knock knock.' Jamie returned carrying a tray and nudged the door open.

'He's feeding.' Kayla couldn't wait to share the news to prove she was capable of doing this job as mother as well as he was doing his as a father so far. It hadn't escaped her notice the baby had been cleaned, changed and smelled of those delicate baby products she'd lined up for his first bath. All without Jamie mentioning he'd done it or expecting some sort of accolade most men expected for doing the smallest of tasks. This was someone used to simply getting on with things.

'Well done, both of you. I thought you might need some sustenance yourself.' He set the tray down on the other side of the bed and handed a cup of herbal tea to Cherry. There was another for Kayla along with a plate of toast and jam. She'd never been so grateful for a snack in her whole life.

'That's very thoughtful, Jamie. Thank you.' She'd have to wait for the baby to finish feeding before she'd get to enjoy it.

'I'll take him, so you can eat.' Anticipating her dilemma, he threw a muslin square over his shoulder and transferred the baby, who was in a milk stupor.

'It looks as though you have everything under control here. Is there anything you'd like me to do? Do you want me to stay the night, Kayla? Jamie?'

It would be easy to say yes and keep her friend here as long as possible. To have her at hand the second she had another wobble in confidence. Although it wasn't going to help her acclimatise into her new role if she had someone doing everything for her.

Kayla did a lot of work with parents after birth to continue providing support whether it was doing household chores or minding baby while they napped. However, she didn't want Jamie to think she couldn't manage. She owed it to Liam, Tom and the baby to be the mother he needed. They'd never wanted strangers involved in raising this child. Now she was the only one left she didn't intend to renege on that. Even if it meant doing it alone.

'I don't think that will be necessary.' It was Jamie who rebuffed Cherry's offer before she had a chance to do it more subtly.

'Kayla?'

Doulas, although not wishing to cause any

unrest between parents, were employed primarily for the mum's benefit. Therefore, it came as no surprise when Cherry deferred to her for confirmation she was in agreement.

'I think I'll be fine for tonight. I'm sure the midwife will be calling around tomorrow to check on us too. If I need anything I can phone you.' She'd keep her phone by the bedside just in case. Cherry and Debbie lived only ten minutes away should she find herself overwhelmed by the prospect of motherhood once she was left alone.

'We'll be fine. Thank you, Cherry.'

'We?' If Jamie thought making some tea and toast was all it took to allow him to bulldoze his way into her life, he was mistaken. Any decisions concerning the baby, or the running of the house, were hers to make alone until he proved she could trust him enough to include him.

'I'm not about to go and leave you here on your own. You've just given birth and you're exhausted. Plus, there's the whole "being the dad" thing. I'd like to spend some time with my son, if that's okay with you?' Jamie thought they'd been making progress up until now. He was doing his best to show her it would be better for her to let him play his part and do this together.

That wasn't to say it was easy for him. He might have raised Tom, but he'd done so after he'd been weaned and potty-trained. The poo-nami he'd dealt with downstairs had made him feel mildly queasy but what kind of dad would he be if he couldn't even change a nappy without supervision?

Mind you, Kayla seemed more impressed by the snack. If such a small act, or thought for her welfare, had become such a big deal it was no wonder she had trust issues. There was no doubt in his mind that Liam and Tom would've looked after her, but now there was no one. With them gone he didn't want her to retreat into isolation. Neither of their brothers would have forgiven him if he walked out on her when she needed him most. He'd simply have to work harder on bonding with her as well as their son.

'I—uh—'

'That sounds great, Dad. You can be on hand for the practical things Kayla needs through the night. Call me, Mama K.' It was beginning to feel as though he had an ally in Cherry when she was pushing for him to be included too. Perhaps he'd been too quick in disparaging her role when Kayla took more notice of her doula than her baby's daddy.

'Mama K' wasn't as peppy as the new nickname suggested as she merely grunted her reluctant acceptance.

'I'll see you out, Cherry. You and junior stay where you are.' He ignored Kayla's scowl, knowing Cherry would have agreed with him on the matter anyway.

It was a picture he'd never known he'd wanted to see but suddenly the image of the mother of his child cradling their son in bed was everything. Regardless that Kayla didn't want anything to do with him, that natural instinct to protect them had already kicked in.

It was probably for the best that they'd never made it into bed that afternoon at the coffee shop. Now he'd seen her give birth to his child they had a special bond. One that couldn't be forgotten about in favour of any desire he might have harboured towards her. He could never bed her now and relegate her to the list of women he'd hope to never cross paths with again in case it developed into something serious. This already was serious. Kayla and the baby were his world now. There was no way he was going to complicate that by letting attraction get in the way of this new family dynamic. He was a dad now and the best thing he could do for his son was be better than his own. That entailed putting aside his own wants and needs to focus on those of his son.

'If there's anything at all you need, don't hesitate to get in touch. I know she's stubborn but hang in there. She needs you more than she'll ever admit to.' With a hug and a kiss on the cheek at the door, Cherry disappeared into the darkness, leaving Jamie as backup for the night.

He trudged back up the stairs, bone-weary but with adrenaline still pumping through him after being called into action. If he was confused about his thoughts and feelings around the birth, he could only imagine what Kayla was going through too. Not that she would ever share it with him, he supposed. Something they'd have to rectify if there was any hope he could give her the support she needed to raise this child between them.

The two were asleep when he crept back into the bedroom. He kicked off his shoes and eased himself onto the mattress with the baby lying between his parents.

'What are you doing?' Kayla snapped her eyes open at once.

'I'm just lying down. I can watch the baby if you want to get some rest.' He thought about the fact he'd crawled into bed beside her without an invitation. Being the baby's father didn't give him the right to do that and he could tell by the dark look Kayla was shooting his way that was what she was thinking too.

'I can go if you'd prefer?' He sat up again before his head managed to touch the pillow.

She hesitated but not for long. 'No. Stay.'

'Thanks.' He rolled over onto his side and rested his head on the inside of his arm, so he could watch his son sleep. Kayla was doing the same.

'I think he has your colouring,' he said, marvelling at the tiny blond eyelashes resting against his pale skin and the tuft of golden hair on his scalp.

'You think?'

'Definitely.'

She smiled at that. Both Kayla and Liam were fair whilst he and Tom were darker. He used to joke with the two men that they looked like an angel and a demon when they stood together.

As much as Jamie would be pleased if their boy resembled his mother more, he hoped to see some resemblance to his own family. A reminder he wasn't alone in the world.

'I hope, somehow, we can see a bit of Liam and Tom in him too. Does that sound stupid?' It seemed Kayla was on the same page as she reached out and lifted the baby's hand on one finger.

'Not at all. That's what I was thinking too. Maybe he'll have that touch of red in his hair I used to tease Tom about.'

'Or Liam's cheeky charm. That one could talk his way out of anything.'

'We'll keep them alive no matter what,' he promised, knowing how important that was to both of them. This child would grow up knowing how amazing his uncles were even though he'd never get to meet them.

'We can't keep calling him "the baby" for ever. It's important he has a name and an identity.'

'What? You're not going for James Junior? JJ for short.'

She shot him down with one of those looks that could wither a rose from a hundred yards. 'No.'

'Seriously though, do you think we should name him after our brothers? William Thomas?'

Kayla wrinkled her nose. 'I don't think it would be fair on him. It would be kind of weird too, calling out my brother's name when he's not here.'

'Good point.' It would probably rip their hearts out to have an everyday reminder of their loss and it wasn't the baby's fault. He shouldn't have to feel guilty he was here when they weren't. Something which surely would have to be explained when he was at an age to understand the circumstances in which he'd been brought into the world.

'What about something they liked?'

'I'm not calling my son Rioja.' They'd both loved to party in their younger days but had settled down in preparation for a parenthood they'd never got to enjoy.

'I was thinking more along the lines of musicals or films.'

'They were both sci-fi geeks. Didn't they meet at that convention?'

'Yeah. They did love their cosplay. I can only imagine the outfits they'd have made for this little one.' That shadow seemed to move in again, clouding over the sunshine that had come into their lives. He supposed it was always going to be this way. Every joy they found in their son was going to be tinged with grief. Unless they could somehow marry the two and be reminded of the fun times they'd had with the guys.

'What about Luke? I vaguely remember a

late-night conversation when they were discussing possible baby names. I think that was one of the ones they'd favoured for a boy.'

'Luke.' Kayla sounded the name on her tongue whilst studying the sleeping babe between them. 'It suits him.'

Her approval of his brainwave made him feel as though he was contributing. He'd take that victory and leave the question over the surname for another day.

'Baby Luke it is, then. When he's old enough we'll do a photo shoot in costume together. We'll make it fun and honour Tom and Liam in our own way.'

'If you think I'm wearing a skintight bodysuit purporting to be some sort of body armour you've got another think coming!'

He hadn't considered that, but now that was all that was on his mind. It would be a boyhood dream come true to have a girlfriend dress up in a superhero outfit. Jamie stopped himself from saying something along those lines and ruining his chance of being part of this family for good. When had he started seeing Kayla in a different light from simply being the oven for his brother's surrogate baby, anyway? Probably around the time they'd first met, and she'd treated him with such unexplained disdain. He'd always enjoyed the company of feisty women when that passion often carried on into the bedroom. Where they were now. With their baby.

'I'll wear the bodysuit, then, and really give us something to laugh about.'

He succeeded in doing just that when she chuckled. 'I'll look forward to it.'

She stopped laughing at his expense and looked so deep into his eyes the mood changed between them again to something more charged. 'Thanks, Jamie.'

'For what?' As far as he could see she was the one who'd done the hard work.

'For being here. Despite my attempts to get rid of you. I'm glad you didn't listen to me.'

'Stubborn, is what Cherry called you.'

'I stand up for what I believe in. I don't think there's anything wrong with that.' She sniffed, not finding any humour in her friend's description.

'Not at all, but not everyone is out to hurt

you either. Some of us simply want what's best for you.'

'That may be true...on this occasion. It doesn't mean you'll get away with it in future.' The warning was there for him not to try and walk over her wishes again in future. He knew better than that, but he wouldn't apologise for stepping in when he deemed it necessary. Like tonight.

'Noted and understood.'

For a while they lay in silence listening to the soft snores of their sleeping son. Jamie was overcome with a surge of gratitude and admiration for the woman whose bed he was sharing. He watched her fight sleep, her eyes fluttering open and closed until they finally shut tight. She was bound to be exhausted and he wasn't going to leave her here to parent alone when there were two of them to share the workload. It was the least he could do in return for the son she'd given him, for the family she'd created with him and for honouring his brother. Best of all, she'd permitted him to be part of her life. An honour he wouldn't take for granted.

He reached out and brushed his knuckles across her cheek, barely touching her warm skin.

'Thank you, Kayla.' He leaned across, careful not to disturb Luke, and placed a kiss where his fingers had touched her cheek. She let out a little moan and snuggled deeper into her pillow with a smile.

For a man who'd sworn off taking on more responsibility in his personal life, he couldn't think of anywhere else he'd rather be than in bed with Kayla and his newborn son.

CHAPTER FIVE

KAYLA WAS HALFWAY between sleep and consciousness. She knew she had to open her eyes, face the day along with her new responsibilities, but sheer exhaustion kept dragging her further down into the bed. She was so delirious she'd even imagined Jamie kissing her last night. It had been so vivid she could still feel the gossamer-light touch of his mouth on her skin.

The show of affection, even in her imagination, had been welcome. It had gone some way to assuaging her fears she was a rubbish mum when she'd spent most of the night feeding, or trying to feed, Luke. Her full, aching breasts were a reminder of why she had to wake.

Those mothering instincts forced her to peel her eyes open. Only to find the other side of the bed empty. She scrabbled to sit up, scouring the room for evidence of her baby.

'Luke? Jamie?' He'd stayed with her through the night, leaving her to feed in private but there for nappy changes and tea-making. Invaluable, but that didn't give him just cause to take her baby away without her consent.

Barefoot, she padded along the landing calling his name, a rising panic fluttering in her chest overshadowing any other physical discomfort.

Jamie had been insistent about being a dad to this baby. What if he'd waited until she'd fallen asleep and taken Luke?

She picked up her pace and started down the stairs. 'Jamie? Have you got my baby?'

He ducked his head out around the living-room door. 'He's in here, sleeping.'

Not even a finger placed on his lips could stop the rage inside Kayla unleashing in a verbal torrent. 'How dare you? How could you scare me like that? You had no right to take him without my say-so.'

Her whole body was shaking as she faced him, standing halfway down the stairs. She should never have gone to sleep and left him with the baby. Luke was her responsibility and Jamie couldn't sneak in and take that from her when he wanted.

Jamie stared back at her, mouth agape, apparently unable to give her an explanation. In her current mood she didn't care how cute he looked with his half-flattened hair, wrinkled shirt and morning stubble. Since she was the mother, she was the one who'd take care of this child on their brothers' behalf.

'I've told you once already to get out of my house. Don't make me say it again.'

Her threat shocked him back to life.

'Kayla, calm down. I only moved him so you could get a better sleep. You were up half the night feeding him.' He didn't reference his own lack of sleep, which was apparent by the dark circles under his eyes, but that didn't make her any more susceptible to his obvious charms.

'That's my job. To feed him.' At the same time she heard the baby wake with a shrill cry, she felt the dampness on the front of her nightdress as her milk came in. Nature proving the point on her behalf. It was impossible for her to deny her responsibility to this child she'd brought into the world.

'I'm not disputing that.' Jamie sighed as she pushed past him at the bottom of the staircase on her way to retrieve her son.

'You don't have to do this on your own, Kayla.'

'I do.' Liam wasn't here any more, and she'd have to get used to that. He'd been her lifeline through childhood, taking punishments on her behalf and deflecting their parents' negative attention from her when needed. If it weren't for him loving her she might have believed she deserved every bad thing that had ever happened to her.

It was him who'd talked her into going to London in the first place, subsidised her through her midwife training and sympathised when the job wasn't what she'd expected. Liam had been the one to get her out of her toxic relationship with Paul and convince her to start the career she wanted as a doula. Now he was gone she'd have to learn to stand on her own two feet. Apart from

Luke, she was alone in the world. For his sake she had to be strong and stop relying on someone who was no longer there.

She lifted Luke out of his basket and undid the front of her nightgown to feed him. Jamie turned away. She knew she could've been more discreet while breastfeeding but this was her home. She shouldn't have to cover up. If he didn't like it, he could leave.

Rather than do that, he stormed across the living-room floor and flopped into an armchair. 'Why does everything have to be a battle between us? You're the most infuriating woman I've ever met.'

'Probably because I won't let you get your own way.' She stroked the top of Luke's head, watching with satisfaction as he fed greedily. It seemed between them they'd figured this thing out.

'This isn't an either-or scenario. We are both his parents and should be working together. I thought we were trying to make this a partnership?' He leaned forward, resting his arms on his knees, his head hanging low. In fact, he looked as defeated as she'd felt not so long ago. If it hadn't been for him giving her a hand in the small hours of the morning she probably wouldn't have slept at all. All he'd been guilty of was doing his best to alleviate some of her burden.

Despite her resistance he was still here. Either he was trying to wear her down to take over when she was at her lowest ebb, or he was being honest about his motives—he simply wanted to be a father to Luke. Something that she didn't have the right to deny either him or her son.

'It's Liam and Tom who should've been here, working together to raise him. When they died, I accepted that I'd have to parent alone. You were never part of the equation, Jamie. By your own choice.'

'Something I've told you is no longer an option for me. I can't walk away from my son. We're going to have to come to an agreement.'

The hairs on the back of Kayla's neck stood up on end at the hint there could be a fight for custody brewing.

'What is it you want, Jamie?' There was no

point dancing around the subject and wasting time. She couldn't dispute the fact he was the father and had rights over his son.

'I want to move in with you. At least until he's settled into some sort of routine.'

That was it? As much as she didn't want him barging into her life, a temporary house-mate would be preferable to being dragged through the courts for access.

'What about work?'

'I'm entitled to paternity leave and I have some holidays to take if necessary. I'll make arrangements with the partners at the clinic.'

'If I agree, it doesn't mean you're entitled to try and take over in here.' She wanted to make that very clear.

'That's not what I want. If one of your clients' husbands said he wanted to help out more, what would you suggest?'

He'd found her Achilles heel, using her own advice against her. There was one way to take advantage of support being offered to new mums, but it involved handing over one of her main jobs as Luke's mother.

'To make sure mum's getting plenty of rest.'

'What could we do to increase the opportunity of rest for you in this situation?'

At the moment she was nothing more than a milk factory for her offspring. It seemed by the time he'd finished a feed it was time for the next one. There was no way of telling if he was getting enough at a time. They couldn't keep on in this fashion for ever. The lack of sleep alone would have her crying over his crib every night beating herself up for failing to keep him satisfied. There was nothing to lose and everything to be gained by dispensing the same advice here as she gave to her clients.

'I could express some milk and you could do some of the feeds.' She conceded defeat and prayed he wouldn't take advantage now he had one foot in the door.

Jamie was going to move in and co-parent with her. Only time would tell if she was doing the right thing in letting that happen. It could be that she'd just invited someone else into her life who'd quash her free will by trying to impose his upon her.

* * *

It had been four weeks since Luke's arrival and Jamie had moved in. His life was as upside down as he'd known it would be upon stepping up as a father. It wasn't as though he hadn't known what he was in for after going through this once before with his little brother. As at that time, he hadn't planned for his life to take that route now either. He hadn't even anticipated staying with Kayla this long. Hell, most of his relationships hadn't lasted this length of time. Apart from the one with Natalie, which had proved he was just as selfish as his father, not taking anyone's feelings into consideration except his own.

However, Kayla had needed him, someone, to share the load with. Sleepless nights and what seemed like a constantly hungry baby had taken a toll and though they were living in the same house they were like zombies barely registering their surroundings at times.

He might have found it easier if they were married and children were something they'd committed to together as husband and wife. If he'd planned his life around having a young family. It was difficult when your world was turned upside down in a heartbeat. Babies weren't something you could return like unwanted gifts.

Now his son was here, of course Jamie wanted him, loved him, and would do anything for him. That didn't mean it was easy. Especially when he was continually trying to prove to Kayla his worth too. It was stress upon layer of stress, but he knew it had to be the same for her too.

She hadn't asked for him to be parachuted into her life either but now they needed to make the most of the situation they were in. Together.

Something she was struggling with, along with trusting him. The concessions she'd made thus far he knew were only because she was exhausted. He was determined to show her he wasn't the man she'd believed he was when they'd first met. Not any more.

'There you go, buster. All clean again.' He picked up from the changing mat the wriggly bundle who was smelling a lot sweeter than he'd done five minutes ago.

Cherry came out of Kayla's room at the same time he left the nursery.

'Hey. Is everything all right?' He was every bit the anxious partner as well as the doting dad. With Luke content and snuggling into his neck, he wished he could do more for Kayla too. The neck snuggling was optional.

'I think she's more like her old self. I'm hoping she's moving past the baby blues, but we'll keep an eye on her.' She wasn't telling him anything he hadn't noticed himself. Kayla had been weepy, which wasn't unusual for new mums with hormones going haywire. Also grieving for her brother, with no other family around to support her. Except for him, who she wasn't overjoyed about having around.

Add to her very emotional circumstances a fussy feeding baby, it was no wonder motherhood hadn't been full of rainbows and unicorns for her so far. It would be easy for a parent to throw their hands up and say they'd had enough, walk away without a backward glance. He thought of his own father, who'd never enjoyed the ups or downs of family life, and realised it said a lot about the strength of a person to hang in there even when parenthood seemed overwhelming. She might not see it now, but he knew Kayla was tougher than his military-trained father. That made her the best mother Luke could want.

'I've taken over doing some of the night feeds, but I think she's a bit resentful of that.' By getting her to express milk so he could bottle-feed Luke, it should've eased some of the pressure on her, but it wasn't working out that way. He'd asked Cherry to come over and have a chat with Kayla since she didn't seem to want to open up to him.

'It's common for new mums to think they've somehow failed by letting a partner help with the feeding. The best thing you can do is to persevere and maybe get her out of the house if you can. Try and get some normality back. I'll pop by for visits when I can too.'

Jamie led her out of the house, her words swirling around his head as he sought an answer as to how best to serve Kayla. The trouble was this wasn't *normal* for either of them.

They were learning how to be a family as they went along.

It would take doing something together, something beneficial to their arrangement, for them to bond. He'd have to think like Kayla to figure out what that might be.

'A baby massage class? Seriously?' If Jamie had suggested they went down to the register office and got married Kayla couldn't have been more surprised.

'I thought it might be good for Luke, and us. It's supposed to help bonding and attachment, as well as a host of other benefits.' He handed her a computer printout as evidence of his covert research.

'I know all about it. I'm just surprised you do. I didn't think you were on board with that sort of *hippy-dippy nonsense*.' Jamie was surprising her more every day. Not least because he was still here, changing nappies, cooking meals and giving bottle feeds when required. They were the actions of a man who simply wanted to do his bit.

Yet, she couldn't bring herself to trust his

motives and be thankful for him being here. To her, it represented her failure as a mother. Luke wasn't settling with the bottle-feeding either.

'It can't do any harm, can it? It will get us out of the house for a while at least.' As he was already strapping Luke into his car seat for the journey, he wasn't leaving her much of a say in the matter.

'My company's that bad, is it?' She hadn't been herself since Luke's birth, but she wasn't likely to be ever again. From now on her every decision, her entire life, revolved around this new arrival.

'No, but we need to introduce this little one to the outside world some time. This is our chance to do some family bonding.'

Family. It was a word, a concept, capable of striking fear and longing into her heart at the same time. She would've loved to have had a family of her own, but her childhood experience had turned it into something to be wary about. It was more than biology, it was that feeling of belonging, love and support she'd had with Liam and Tom.

She didn't know if the significance of the word was the same for Jamie or if it was merely a throwaway comment.

Instead of dwelling on it, she chose to focus on the bonding aspect of the classes he'd joined on their behalf. 'They do say that the one-to-one time during baby massage helps parents recognise their baby's needs. I'm willing to try anything which will make me a better mother.'

It was an insight into her vulnerability she hadn't intended to share but one he'd surely seen for himself recently.

Jamie stopped packing the changing bag with baby essentials to look at her. 'What on earth would make you say such a thing?'

Kayla fussed around Luke, making sure he was well covered before they transferred him out into Jamie's car.

'Let's face it, the breastfeeding hasn't exactly been a resounding success.' If it had been she wouldn't have conceded so easily to the idea of him moving in.

Jamie let the bag fall from his shoulder and walked over to her. She didn't want to make a big deal of this with him and wished she'd kept it to herself in case he used it as ammunition against her later. He rested his hands on her shoulders, the importance of touch reaching home when the gentle pressure was a reminder someone was there for her. Even if it wasn't the brother she'd shared so much with. The only person who'd ever truly loved her.

'You are an amazing mum. Don't ever think different. You've fought for everything you believed best for Luke.'

'That hasn't always worked out either, has it?' She thought of the home birth, which could've gone so wrong, and the breastfeeding, which had. The shame was so great she couldn't look him in the eye. She was a fraud who'd made out she was the expert when, really, she had no clue when it came to raising her own baby.

'Hey.' He cupped her face in his hands and forced her to look at him. The concern for her, the sincerity she saw in his eyes, were unexpected. Perhaps she'd expected him to gloat, or, as she'd seen with other partners, pretend there was nothing wrong.

In that moment she wanted him to hug her, kiss her softly and reassure her everything was going to be all right. The way she'd been imagining him doing in her dreams these past weeks.

'That's enough of that talk. Where's my ballsy earth mother who'd walk over hot coals before letting anything defeat her?'

It was kind of nice that was how he saw her. Dared she say it, even complimentary?

'She's here somewhere. Under layers of baby sick and mum tum.' To say she wasn't at her best was an understatement. She was always telling her new mums not to be so hard on themselves and not to worry about stretch marks and weight gain when they'd just produced another human. It was different when you saw the changes in your own body.

In the scheme of things her appearance was the least of her worries, but she wasn't herself any more. She was aware of that every time she glanced in a mirror. It didn't help her self-esteem knowing Jamie was witness to her gradual decay. His comment highlighted the fact he'd noticed the changes himself. How could he not?

'Kayla, Kayla, Kayla. What am I going to do with you?'

It was a rhetorical question but, when he was still touching her, her mind went to some interesting places regarding what she wanted him to do with her.

A quiver of desire shook her body and for a split second she thought she saw a flicker of interest cross his face too. Then Luke squawked a reminder that he was there, and reality hit home. How could anyone be interested in a woman with unwashed hair wearing yesterday's dirty clothes?

She pulled away, suddenly self-conscious and feeling foolish. Hormones. They could be blamed for everything. Along with the amount of time she was spending with him. He was right. They did need to get out of the house.

'Ignore me. That's what you should do.' She lifted the baby carrier with an *Oof.* Her tiny son was heavier than he appeared.

'That's not something easily done,' he muttered under his breath as he reached out and took the weight from her. 'You shouldn't be straining yourself. No arguments.'

She didn't dare when he swung the baby so easily with one muscular arm. They needed a crowded-room intervention before she started having fantasies about all his other body parts too. Her permanent state of exhaustion lately had curtailed her less than platonic thoughts about him. When she was awake, at least. Her dreams, on the other hand, had become so X-rated it was difficult to separate them from reality. More so when he was parading around her house half naked in the mornings.

'I guess it's time for master Luke to make his introduction into the big wide world. Baby massage, here we come.'

This was about her son, their bond and doing whatever she could to make him happy. It was not a turning point in her relationship with Jamie simply because it was his idea. Or because her body was reminding her there was more to her than being a mum. She was a hot-blooded woman too.

CHAPTER SIX

'WELCOME, EVERYONE. As you may or may not be aware, baby massage is an ancient tradition. It's not simply a new trend the hipsters have latched onto.' As the instructor, Jocelyn, addressed the class, Kayla gave Jamie the side-eye. She knew he'd only done this for her, not because he believed it would be of any use to them.

He kept his gaze straight ahead, but the corner of his mouth tilted up in amusement.

'We're here to promote health and security in our babies. Massage has been known to aid sleep, circulate and alleviate digestive conditions. Best of all, it provides a relaxing experience for baby and parent, reducing stress. So, if you'd like to get started you can lay baby down and lay them on the towels you've hopefully brought with you.'

'Here goes nothing.' Jamie took a couple of towels from the changing bag and spread them out on the wooden floor, leaving Kayla to remove Luke's bumblebee-embellished sleep suit. The room was sufficiently warm she didn't have concerns he'd be too cold.

'Please don't worry if baby needs to be fed or changed during the class. They're our priority here so do what you have to to make them comfortable without judgement.' The woman taking the class did her best to calm the fears of any anxious parents and Kayla was glad she wasn't the only one who might be out of her depth here.

'He's been fed, winded and changed but I can't guarantee he'll enjoy this.' She was surprised to find she was the more sceptical one about what this was going to do other than stress her out if she wasn't doing it right.

'We've got nothing to lose.' Jamie shrugged, and she prayed he was right.

'Okay, mums and dads, we're going to start with the legs. Using a little of the oil you have, I want you to wrap your hands around baby's thigh and, with one hand at a time, pull down in a "milking" motion.' Now that did sound weird even to Kayla's ears.

Her raised eyebrow was mirrored by Jamie's, with added smirk. Nevertheless, she performed the massage on both of Luke's legs.

'Good. Now moving on to the feet, gently rotate each one this way and that. With your thumb I want you to stroke the top of the foot right down to the toes. Then, trace circles over the soles of the feet. Finally, we're going to take each toe between our finger and thumb and stroke those too.'

Luke was slippery beneath Kayla's fingers, but he seemed content lying there as she caressed him. She could hear some babies complaining and the instructor encouraged the mums to cuddle them until they settled back down again. There was a small burgeon of pride that they were doing okay compared to a few of the others present.

Jamie was kneeling beside them on the wooden floor, observing and whispering encouragement to her and Luke. It didn't seem fair to leave him on the periphery when he was the father, and this had been his idea.

'Why don't you do his arms?' she suggested as they were asked to repeat the process.

'Are you sure?' He confirmed she was happy in him participating before he shuffled over on his knees and squeezed a few drops of oil onto his hands. As he massaged their son's dainty arms Kayla was aware of the size of him in comparison. Those large hands enveloping the tiny limbs, capable of doing so much damage, were nothing but tender and loving. Her stress levels were reducing by the second watching him soothe their baby.

So much so, she let him carry on with the chest massage they were given instructions for too.

'Stroke your hands out over baby's chest. With a flat palm at the top of his chest, stroke gently downwards.'

Kayla was mesmerised by Jamie's rhythmic actions and his concentration. This wasn't a demonstration to impress her, or a bid to fool her into thinking he was someone he wasn't. This was a father caring for his baby. She'd seen much of it these last weeks, as well as his kindness towards her. The issue of their baby's surname and his father's details on the birth certificate had yet to be addressed but every day she spent with him earned him a more permanent place in his son's life.

'Jamie, I think—' Her attempt to broach the subject was interrupted as their baby took direct aim at Jamie's chest with a forceful stream of urine.

'Luke! Really?' There wasn't much Jamie could do other than stem the flow with a hastily positioned towel, but his once white T-shirt was already stained with baby pee.

'It proves he's definitely relaxed,' she pointed out in between peals of laughter.

'Glad to see you two are enjoying it.' His wide smile said he was being genuine, and the incident hadn't bothered him at all.

Although, Kayla wouldn't have minded if he'd felt the need to strip off too. Living together had provided numerous opportunities for her to view him *sans* shirt. The sight of a toned male torso wasn't something she'd thought she needed in her life until it had become the highlight of her morning. Such a contrast to the barely-made-it-out-of-bed-today look she offered in return.

She tossed him a pack of baby wipes and a clean towel. 'Dry yourself off and I'll take over with our little piddler.'

'I swear you two planned this behind my back.' He dabbed at the stain on his shirt, giving them a mock scolding. It was clear Jamie was going to be a pushover when it came to their son for real. She wasn't sure she'd be any better when she adored him so much.

'We wouldn't do anything to embarrass Daddy, would we, Luke?' It was the first time she'd assigned him the title out loud and the world hadn't ended. Accepting Jamie as Luke's father was the right thing to do. More than that, it was good to know she had someone to share all this with. She wasn't alone after all.

As she turned Luke over to massage his back, there was a gentle pressure on hers as Jamie rested his hand on her. 'You don't know how much it means to hear you say that.'

That delicious tingle of awareness that accompanied his touch reached up to tickle the back of her neck.

'I've been thinking about making it official. It's about time we registered Luke's birth, don't you think?' She scooped up the now sleepy source of their amusement and love and faced his father.

'I would absolutely love that.' Jamie's eyes were sparkling with bright tears, the move as significant to him as it was to her.

There was no going back now. Once he was named on the birth certificate Jamie would be part of Luke's life for ever. And hers.

Jamie was on cloud nine as they left the class. Despite his son christening his new T-shirt. The class had gone better than he'd ever expected when it had prompted Kayla into a conversation about the birth certificate. When she'd first called him 'Daddy' when talking to Luke, he'd have sworn his heart stopped momentarily at the shock. This was getting real. He'd achieved what he'd set out to do and ensured his place in Luke's upbringing.

With that came a lifetime duty to take care of his son.

He'd been so hell-bent on getting Kayla to accept him as Luke's father and cement a place in his life, he wondered if he'd really considered the implications. Once his name was on the birth certificate it was official. He was a dad. The consequences of not being a good enough parent were something he'd lived with his entire life because of the selfish actions of his father. He wouldn't intentionally do anything to hurt Luke but the onus on him to be a better father than his own weighed heavily on his heart.

That carefree existence he'd anticipated once Tom had become independent was now a thing of the past. He hadn't thought much about his own future beyond making up for his lost youth. Now the only one available to him was here with Kayla and Luke. He hoped it was enough for him. That he was enough for them.

'What's all the noise?' Kayla drew his attention away from self-pity back to the cacophony of sound out in the hallway liable to undo their hard work in getting Luke to sleep.

'It's probably the next class. Baby yoga. I looked into that too, but we'll have to wait until Luke's older and you've had your six-week check-up.' He'd researched lots of classes before he'd settled on baby massage. It had been hard work finding something to suit them that was also something he was willing to participate in. When Kayla was up to it she might join some of those singing classes where they all sat in a circle singing nursery rhymes to oblivious infants, but he wasn't that much of a happy-clappy chappie. At least not in public.

'You'd be willing to do yoga with us?' Her incredulity at the prospect after he'd demonstrated he was prepared to do almost anything for them hurt feelings he wasn't aware he had. Here he was committing the rest of his life to looking after his son, yet Kayla clearly still didn't trust him to stick around. After a month of her getting to know him, seeing him doing his best for this family, he expected her to think better of him. Otherwise what was the point of him being here?

'Sure. I'll order up some yoga pants specially,' he said, with a lot less enthusiasm than he'd had when he'd started this quest for a family-bonding activity.

'Now that I'd like to see.' Her interest in seeing him in the unforgiving tight fabric stopped him from wallowing too much.

'You would?' His spirits lifted further as she blushed ferociously, realising what she'd said. Perhaps she had been paying him more attention than she'd led him to believe.

'I'm joking. Is it getting hot in here? Maybe we should get out of this stuffy room.' The more she bustled around Luke, collecting his belongings and pretending she hadn't encouraged Jamie to parade around in skintight pants, the funnier he found it.

'Maybe we should stay. I could strip down to my boxers and you could watch me do the downward dog, if that's what you're into.' It seemed so long ago when he'd teased her at the wedding, but now he remembered why he'd enjoyed it so much. He made her flustered and to him that suggested she wasn't impervious to that attraction he'd felt towards her since day one. Perhaps, subconsciously, that was part of the reason he'd agreed to participate in the surrogacy when it cemented a connection between them they might have otherwise avoided.

She tutted but didn't outright dismiss the idea.

By the time they were ready to leave, the rest of their class had already gone, and the new attendees were filing in. It was a much more animated and vocal group who replaced their sedate gathering. Mostly down to the age of the younger participants, who were mobile and giving their parents the runaround.

'I think the object of this class might be to tire the kids out, along with all that well-being and inner-calmness stuff.' The chaos of temper tantrums and crawling, falling little ones was a scary insight into what the future held for them. He could see the same realisation in Kayla's wide eyes as she watched it unfold around them too.

'Fingers crossed it works, for the sake of their poor mothers.' It was obvious her focus was on the harassed parents chasing their offspring and trying to get them to sit on the mats provided for the session.

Jamie noticed there were several using reins, with one end tethered to the child and the other around the mother's wrist so they didn't wander too far. He thought they'd be better using one of those retractable dog leads instead. Then the rug rats could be reeled in at the touch of a button. He didn't share that thought with Kayla in case she deemed it inappropriate and saw the joke as a gauge of his parenting skills.

'At least we only have one to contend with.' His eye had been drawn to the twins in the corner who had hared off in different directions as soon as they'd come through the double doors. Little blond heads bobbed up and down as one jumped on the yoga mats whilst the other picked something up off the floor.

'Lena, sweetheart, what have you got in your mouth? Let Mummy see.' Lena's mother edged cautiously towards her daughter as though approaching a skittish fawn, then launched herself like a lioness to wrestle the unidentified object from her cub's mouth.

'Goodness. You'd need eyes in the back of your head to manage those two.' Kayla followed their escapades, her head turning left and right as though she were at a tennis match.

'Yeah. Maybe I should go and see if she needs a hand.' If he and Kayla were finding aspects of parenthood hard to handle, he could only imagine what it was like to have two toddlers and apparently no one to help out. He was sure the rewards outweighed the parenting trials, as he was finding out for himself, but that didn't mean a person couldn't use a hand sometimes.

He set the baby carrier beside Kayla and headed towards the mother to offer his assistance, hoping she wouldn't be as offended as the mother of his son tended to be when he wanted to help.

It was on his mind whether or not to introduce himself as a GP or a parent when there was a loud thud from the far side of the room.

'Billy!'

'Jamie!'

Both mum and Kayla drew his attention to the hurdling tot who'd been temporarily left unsupervised.

They all ran towards the child, who was lying motionless on the floor. Jamie winced as he realised that thud had been his head hitting the hard wood. It had been loud enough to stop all the other chatter in the room as everyone else looked on in horror.

'Billy? Someone help me. He's not breathing.' The distraught mother was kneeling over her unconscious child, with the other one caught under her arm. She attempted to lift him up and Jamie was quick to step in.

'Stop! Don't move him. Let me assess him first.' He could see the fear flicker in the mother's eyes and she was frozen, unsure of what to do.

'Jamie's a doctor. He knows what he's doing.' Kayla gently encouraged the mother to come away and let him get on with examining her son.

'Billy? Can you hear me? My name's Jamie.

I'm a doctor. I need you to open your eyes for me.' There was no response. He was careful in tilting the child's head back and lifting his chin in case there was a neck injury but opening his airways took priority. There was no chest movement and no sign, or sound, of him breathing. He turned to the women standing close by. 'I'm going to have to perform CPR.'

He didn't have time to react to the anguished cries of the mother, but Kayla had that in hand as she reassured her everything would be okay.

'Everyone, I think it would be best if you all go outside. We don't want to upset the other children.' She addressed the room too whilst Jamie started rescue breaths.

Jamie pinched Billy's nose closed between his finger and thumb and opened his mouth a fraction. With a deep breath, he placed his lips around the child's, making a tight seal. He blew and watched the little chest rise. When he broke the seal, he watched the chest fall again as it would if the child were breathing normally. Jamie took another breath and repeated the process.

He heard Jocelyn, the instructor, shoo everyone out of the door and footsteps as she walked over to the scene.

'I've phoned for an ambulance. Let me take these little ones out of your way so you can focus on Billy.' There was no objection from Kayla or the other mother as she walked away carrying Luke and holding Lena's hand.

'This isn't working.' The five rescue breaths hadn't done anything to get him breathing on his own again.

Unprompted, Kayla knelt down beside him and began chest compressions. Positioning herself above the baby, and with her arm straight, she placed the heel of her hand on the lower part of the breastbone. Making sure the pressure wasn't applied over the ribs, she pushed down.

They exchanged glances. No words were needed for him to know she was thinking the same thing as him. They needed to save this child's life. It could easily have been their own baby. Would they be so calm then and able to provide the same medical assistance?

Jamie had known from the second he'd become a father it wasn't only his personal life that would be affected, it was going to influence his work too. He would relate better to every overwrought parent who came to him worried about their own health or that of their children. Each child he treated now he was going to compare to his own son and what he would do in the same circumstances. Being a father would make him a better man and a better doctor all because of Luke. A child he wouldn't have if not for Kayla and their brothers.

'No sign of life,' Kayla confirmed as she ended the round of compressions and he got ready to perform more rescue breaths.

'Let me know if you want me to take over.' He knew how exhausting it could be to continue CPR until an ambulance arrived; he'd had to do it several times over the course of his career. There was no telling what experience of this situation Kayla had. It was easy to think her work as a midwife and a doula only involved delivering babies. Whilst childbirth in this day and age wasn't as risky as it had been in previous decades, there could still be serious complications. All of which Kayla had demonstrated she could cope with, given this life-or-death situation she was handling so professionally.

On a personal note, it was nice to have that physical and mental support. He was so used to doing things on his own—from raising Tom, grieving for him and even down to working out of his own office in the clinic—it was a wonderful new experience.

A partner wasn't something he'd ever really considered. He figured another person in his life would simply entail more responsibility, more demands on his time. Kayla was beginning to show him there were benefits to having someone to share these moments with. It reminded him he wasn't alone and gave them a common bond they could chat about together later. Letting another person into his life might not be as bad as he'd always imagined. He wanted to make Kayla feel the same way when it came to raising Luke.

Despite this new revelation, Jamie was still aware of Billy's mother sobbing nearby, Kayla counting with every compression, and, more importantly, the sirens outside in the distance.

'Checking for signs of life present.' He called it before they repeated the process, praying they could get him breathing on his own rather than simply keeping his heart circulating blood around his body.

As they sat back Jamie tried to block out the white noise around him and listened for any gasping, watched for any movement. Slowly, Billy's chest began to rise and fall by itself. He checked his pulse and the sense of relief to feel it beating faintly against his fingers made him choke on the emotions of a new dad saving the life of someone else's baby.

'He's breathing!' Kayla spotted the signs too and quickly passed the information on to the anxious mother.

Between them Jamie and Kayla turned Billy onto his side, into the recovery position, and continued to monitor his breathing in case they had to administer further CPR.

'Mummy's here, sweetheart.' The mum sat down beside the child and stroked his forehead, tears streaming down her face. Kayla put her arm around the woman's shoulders and squeezed. Jamie could see she was crying too. He wasn't far from it himself. Later, when the shock kicked in and he was nursing his own son to sleep, reality would probably hit home. At least on this occasion he had someone who'd gone through it with him to talk it over and process what had happened.

'The paramedics will take over from here and get him to the hospital for a check-up,' he managed to croak out, his throat dry and aching from trying to hold it together.

'I'm sure he's going to be fine. Jamie and I will call the hospital later and find out how you're all doing.'

'I can't thank you enough. I dread to think what would've happened if you hadn't—' The woman's voice cracked as she contemplated the consequences.

'We *were* here and he's breathing on his own again. Everything's going to be all right.' Jamie didn't have to spend too long convincing her as the paramedics came rushing in to tend to their tiny patient.

He and Kayla got to their feet and let the

crew take over once they'd passed on the relevant information concerning Billy's condition. They were both in a hurry to get out to their own son to check up on him, but it was fair to say they were both a tad unsteady on their feet now the adrenaline was subsiding and shock was setting in. All the other parents had left, with only the class instructor remaining, holding Lena's hand and carrying Luke in the other.

'I thought it would be best to send everyone home.'

'Good call. There's no point in getting the other kids distressed. I doubt anyone would want to go ahead after that anyway.' There was no way people would manage to be serene and do a yoga class after that. It was going to take quite a while for him to calm down and get his heart rate under control.

'Billy's going to be okay. We got him breathing on his own but they're going to take him in the ambulance to the hospital just in case.' Kayla swung Luke up into her arms and snuggled into him. Jamie would wait his turn, but he wanted that physical contact with his son too for reassurance he was safe.

'Oh, thank goodness.' Their temporary babysitter clutched at her chest. 'I have first-aid training myself but I'm glad we had professional medics present to save him.'

The ambulance crew came past with Billy's mother following close behind. 'Thanks, everyone, for all your help. I'll take Lena with me to the hospital. Their dad's going to meet me there.'

'Take care,' Kayla called after them as Lena tottered off hand in hand with her mother, clutching the lollipop that Jocelyn must have given her to pacify her during all the drama. At least the twins would have two parents at the hospital to share the responsibilities. He guessed childcare was something he and Kayla were going to have to figure out around their work schedules. Although, she'd probably be taking as much maternity leave as she could for now.

'I think I'll go and make us all a strong, sugary cup of tea. We need it.' Jocelyn got no argument from him but as Kayla was about to voice her objection, he stepped in.

'Caffeine and sugar for the shock. Doctor's orders.' Then they could go home as a family and thank their lucky stars they all had each other.

CHAPTER SEVEN

WHAT KAYLA WAS realising about parenthood was that she had to set aside any impending meltdown and continue with the baby's schedule as normal. Rather than hyperventilating over what they'd been part of at the yoga class, she had to feed Luke, give him his bath and put him down for the night before she could even analyse what had happened.

'That's what I call a mad day,' she said as she dropped down onto the sofa beside Jamie.

'It was intense.' Jamie kicked off his shoes and opened the takeaway cartons sitting on the coffee table in front of them. The healthy-eating plan had taken a back seat these past days as they got used to their new routine. Although Jamie had been cooking for her, and it was tasty, it wasn't her usual menu. It was a stretch too far to expect him to cook tonight too when the events of the day had left them both drained. He'd gone out for Chinese food instead and as she sucked up the noodles in her vegetable chow mein she was glad they'd decided on a takeaway. It gave them some much-needed time out for the rest of the evening.

'And scary. I'm glad Billy's going to be okay. Thanks for phoning the hospital and checking up on him. I don't think I would have slept otherwise.' Even though he'd been breathing on his own, there was always that worry something could happen and his condition could deteriorate. The reassurance could tick one thing off her worry list even if there were other things troubling her.

'Nor me. I think I've got new-dad hormones going on.' Nothing seemed to be affecting his appetite as he helped himself to a huge forkful of unidentified meat in an unnatural red sauce.

'Really? You were so cool today, as though you weren't fazed at all.' The way he'd dealt with the emergency so confidently and efficiently, she'd convinced herself that getting upset about a patient was unprofessional of her. It was Jamie's stoicism that had got her through the incident when she'd been thinking about Luke the whole time they'd been trying to revive Billy.

'Are you kidding me? Life or death isn't something I take a casual attitude towards. I had a job to do—it was simple as that. Remember, it was you who did the chest compressions, and he wouldn't have come back if not for that too.'

'It was a team effort, I suppose. It's just… you seem to be doing so much better as a dad than I am as a mum.'

'How do you figure that one out?' He set his cutlery down and frowned at her, waiting for her to explain herself and expose her weakness.

'You've had experience with Tom and you've dealt with the dirty nappies and feeds better than I have.' It took a lot to admit that to him and open up about how useless she thought she was in comparison. To have him laugh in her face wasn't something she was prepared for.

'Is that what you really think? Listen, I was Tom's big bro, not his parent. I might've been the one to cook his dinner and take him to school, but I certainly wasn't on call during the baby years. As for the rest, I messed up there too sometimes. I didn't know how to raise a child any more then than I do now. That first night with Luke, man, that was a steep learning curve. I think the world fell out of his backside. His clothes were so badly stained I had to throw them out. I cleaned him up and put a new sleep suit on him so you wouldn't think I was incompetent. It was important to me that you thought I was up to the job.' He ducked his head and looked up at her with those big brown eyes.

It was her turn to laugh, but more out of disbelief that he'd been as out of his depth as she'd been. 'Why have we been torturing ourselves pretending that we know what we're doing?'

'I can only speak for myself here, but I was afraid if I didn't measure up you'd give me my marching orders.'

It wasn't an outlandish notion when she'd

been so hostile towards him and resentful of his position in her son's life. 'I'm sorry I made you feel like that. I know what it's like to live under a constant threat.'

She took a sip of her water, her mouth dry at the mere thought of her parents. Jamie deserved an explanation of her behaviour when it had been misdirected at him at what should have been the happiest time of his life. 'My mum and dad were very strict. I don't know if Liam ever discussed them with you?'

He shook his head. 'All Tom told me was that they'd disowned him when he told them he was gay, and he didn't like to talk about them. So I didn't. I figured that kind of people weren't worth wondering about.'

One thing in Jamie's favour was that he didn't have a homophobic bone in his body. It was refreshing after growing up in a small village where Liam had been constantly gossiped about and shunned when they were younger. 'Trust me, they're not.'

'I take it you're not in contact with them any more? They weren't at the memorial service.'

'As a rule, I don't have anything to do with them. My conscience got the better of me though, and I did phone to let them know about the accident. They made it very clear that they didn't care.' The emotion of that conversation, at least on her part, threatened to spill out again. Her throat was raw as she fought to quell the bitterness back inside. Jamie didn't need to know they'd said their brothers had died because of their 'sinning'.

'I'm so sorry. That must've been a hard call to make.'

'The worst,' she said through a strained smile.

'Do they know about Luke?' It was a reasonable assumption that a child's grandparents would want to be part of his life, but her parents weren't reasonable or kind. Nor were they the kind of people either of them would want in their son's life.

'No. I swore that day I'd never contact them again. Trust me, you wouldn't want them anywhere near Luke. My father ruled with a firm hand, my mother with a cruel tongue. Between them they kept us terrified in case we did anything to upset them. That's why I was so against you being involved. I don't want anyone to have control of me like that ever again. You seemed like a threat to that, barging in and demanding access to your son.'

'I had no idea. I'm so sorry. Losing Tom was like the end of the world and I just wanted something, someone to cling onto. I wanted my family back.' He stared at his hands and Kayla knew he was thinking about his brother and all the things they would no longer do together. She did it herself every time someone mentioned Liam.

'That was why I agreed to the surrogacy. I couldn't see that I would ever find a man I'd completely trust to enter into that kind of serious relationship where I'd want a child with him. I made the mistake of getting involved with someone who took advantage of my history. He manipulated me and changed me into someone I didn't recognise. Someone weak who was desperate to please him with no thought to her own needs. It's been hard for me to trust myself, never mind another man. This was supposed to be the easy way out.'

She'd been naïve. They all had. A baby was a serious commitment and a responsibility for life. He wasn't going to solve all of her issues with her parents and the control they'd exerted over her. It was down to her to move past it all so her son wasn't tainted by her legacy. She didn't want Luke growing up afraid to love, or share his life with someone, because that was what she instilled in him.

'I'm sorry, Kayla, and I can understand that to some extent.' Jamie scooped up some rice along with the bright red concoction, leaving Kayla waiting for him to finish so she could hear how he related to her tragic lack of love life. From everything she'd heard, Jamie Garrett was never short of a woman in his bed. That was part of the reason she was wary of getting into any sort of a relationship with him. Even a platonic one. She hadn't seen the point in setting up a family dynamic if he'd take off the next time a woman caught his eye. However, he'd shown a commitment to

Luke these past days that went beyond mere bragging rights.

She watched him swallow, then take another forkful of food. Unlike him, she couldn't eat another mouthful until she heard the rest of this story explaining what made him him. 'I don't know much about your personal background except that your parents passed away when Tom was young.'

He took the hint to continue and paused with the food halfway to his mouth. 'They weren't bad people. Dad was in the army so we didn't see that much of him. Even when he was on leave he was an outdoorsy kind of guy. You know, he went away on hiking trips a lot. He was a bit of a loner and probably shouldn't have had kids. He had a climbing accident, broke his neck in a fall. Mum died about five years later when Tom was eleven. She had a stroke and never recovered.'

'That's horrible. I'm so sorry. You were all so young.' It sounded as though the family had been blighted by tragedy and now he'd lost Tom too. Life could be so fragile, and unfair. She'd found that out with her brother's death. Even though she didn't have a relationship with her parents, she could understand how great a loss Jamie had suffered to date. It was a testament to him that he'd been able to carry on when they'd been orphaned and assume guardianship of his brother when he'd been barely an adult himself.

'There was never really any time to process each event. After my dad's death I stepped up to be the man of the house, keeping Tom in line and taking care of bills and things. When Mum went it was only natural I took on both parenting roles. Losing Tom has been the toughest time of my life. I'm not sure I'll ever get over it.' He pushed his food away, his appetite apparently leaving, and Kayla knew it was her fault for bringing up painful memories.

'I'm not sure we're supposed to. Death changes the people left behind but I think it's important we carry on and live the life our loved ones never got to have.' She expected Luke was going to make that easier. With a child in her life she had no choice but to carry on for his sake and get up each morning to start afresh. Her mind might take a while to catch up in leaving the past behind, but outwardly she was determined to try.

'I can't help thinking that I wasn't there for Tom when he needed me most. Perhaps I was too giddy about the idea of being a single man free of responsibilities to think about the danger he and Liam were putting themselves in out there. I should've warned them what they were doing was reckless, instead of celebrating my bachelor status. Even though he was a grown man, I don't think I stopped taking care of him until he and Liam got married.'

'There was nothing you could have done, Jamie. They wanted one last adventure before they settled into family life and we wouldn't have begrudged them that. What happened was a tragedy, an accident that no one could have foreseen.' She'd torn herself apart too, wondering if she could've done anything to prevent their deaths, but no amount of guilt or apportioning blame was going to bring them back.

'I was too self-involved. At that time of my life I wasn't taking anyone's feelings, other than my own, into consideration. Including yours. I'm sorry for the way I behaved at the wedding. My ego got a little out of control for a while there, realising I was still attractive to the opposite sex despite my advancing years.'

'You're hardly ancient.' She didn't want to tell him there was no need to apologise when his forthright manner at the wedding had awakened emotions, sensations in her she'd given up on ever having again. Once she'd realised relationships were never going to work out for her, she'd thought she'd shut them off, considered them a waste of energy. Clashing with Jamie at the wedding had made her realise she wasn't dead from the neck down.

Perhaps having her eyes opened to the fact she was still open to a man's attentions had scared her into the surrogacy deal. Knowing once she was pregnant her focus would be completely on the baby and she wouldn't leave herself vulnerable to another doomed romance. That had been her get-out plan. Until their brothers had died and brought Jamie back into her universe, along with that resurfacing chemistry it was getting harder to deny lingering between them.

'Why, thank you.' He smoothed his hair back with his hand, feigning an arrogance she now knew wasn't the real Jamie.

'You're handsome, single, with a medical career. Why wouldn't women find you attractive?' Despite trying to be casual, she felt her cheeks burning with the heat of the admission she was one of those women.

'Wow. So many compliments tonight. You'll make me blush.'

It was Kayla who was blushing furiously as he teased her. She tried to play it cool with a roll of the eyes. 'I'm serious. Are you telling me you haven't had your fair share of advances from smitten women over the years?'

'I didn't say that.'

Was it her imagination or were his cheeks a little pinker than usual? Kayla experienced a twinge of jealousy imagining a string of gorgeous women chatting up the father of her baby. It was possible this living together and raising a child had fostered the idea in her head that they were in some sort of fantasy relationship when, really, circumstances had forced them together. There was no reason she should have any claim on him when he wouldn't be within a hundred miles of her if not for their son.

'Yet you never sought to get married and have a family of your own. Why now?'

'When Tom was growing up I didn't want him to take second place the way we had when our dad was alive. I was dating someone, Natalie, but I didn't have the time or energy to commit long-term. Inevitably she got hurt when she realised marriage wasn't on the cards even though we weren't more than kids ourselves. Since then I've found a brief dalliance here and there avoids the drama. I wasn't a monk, but for a while there I was going through some sort of delayed adolescence. The one I missed out on.'

It was a heartfelt admission on Jamie's part that he had been the playboy she'd suspected, at least for a while. The important question on Kayla's mind now was which Jamie she was currently shacked up with, because there was only one of those characters she was interested in having around.

'So, you're back in parenting mode…but what happens when you do meet the woman of your dreams? Will Luke remain your top priority?' She didn't want her son to suffer for the sake of his father's libido should he lapse back into his Lothario alter ego, or if he started a new family with a woman he truly loved.

'I have no plans for any more children,' he answered with a lopsided smile. 'Even if I did, I can promise you Luke will always be my number one.' He said it with such sincerity and conviction she believed it. Whilst she was glad for Luke's sake he would always have his father, she was heart-sore that there was no mention of her in his priorities. She wasn't his partner in a romantic way but, as co-parent, she would still be part of his life in some form. Whilst it didn't seem relevant to him, she was already coming to terms with having him around. She'd miss him if he suddenly met someone else and relegated his parenting duties to unsupervised weekend visits.

'I'm kinda getting used to having you around,' she confessed, in case he was still in any doubt about that.

'Good.' He held her gaze a fraction too long until the hairs on the back of her neck began to stand to attention, her body flirting with the idea his interest in her might go beyond their mutual offspring after all.

She glanced away first, her imagination doing nothing to make her life any easier. Jamie might not seek to control her, but neither was she going to let emotions or desire dictate her actions.

'I'll take these away—'

'Why don't I tidy these up—?'

They both reached for the discarded takeaway cartons on the table at the same time. Their hands accidentally grabbed one another but it was some time before either let go. Kayla's heart skittered in her chest, barely taking the time to fully form each beat. How desperate it would make her appear for affection if she turned into a Regency era heroine who swooned at the mere touch of a man's hand.

'Be my guest. I think I'll go on to bed.

Don't worry about waiting up. I'll take the first shift with Luke and you can get some sleep.' Somewhere that wasn't her bedroom. A place where she wouldn't be sleeping any time soon.

'If you insist. It has been a long day.' He didn't argue the way he usually did, always elevating her need for rest above his. Perhaps he was keen to get away before she did make a scene and embarrass herself.

Kayla didn't hang around to dissect her reaction to him any further. Instead she peeped in on Luke, who was still sleeping soundly, and retrieved her nightdress from under her pillow. She disappeared into the bathroom to change into the strappy, satin nightgown she'd taken to wearing instead of her mumsy nightdress. It was cooler and made her feel more like a woman than a mere baby machine. She almost convinced herself it was nothing to do with how she looked to Jamie as she brushed her hair in the mirror until it shone.

Teeth brushed, and with her recently removed clothes in her arms, she opened the

bathroom door and ran straight into Jamie.
A bare-chested Jamie, clad only in boxers.

Her carefully folded pile of laundry tumbled to the floor as she came face-to-pecs
with his smooth, taut, hypnotic torso.

'Sorry, I didn't realise you were in there.'
He seemed genuinely surprised to run into
her, but he didn't step back to let her past. His
eyes travelled over her bare shoulders, assessing her new look, and when his gaze dipped
down into the V of her black chemise Kayla
was powerless to disguise her reaction this
time. Her nipples hardened into tight buds,
swollen against the silky fabric and garnering further attention.

'I'm finished now. It's bedtime. For me, I
mean.' By spelling out the sleeping arrangements she'd simply guided him to where her
own thoughts were headed.

'Well, goodnight, then.' As though it were
a nightly tradition, Jamie dipped his head to
place a kiss on her lips. Kayla stood up on
her tiptoes, keen to receive it.

Eyes closed, she revelled in the slight brush
of his mouth against hers. It reminded her of

those gentle kisses of reassurance she'd enjoyed in her dreams, night after night.

'Night,' she said when it ended, forced to open her eyes and come back down to earth.

Jamie didn't move, his eyes still trained on her mouth and the atmosphere between them crackled with awareness and desire. She was frozen to the spot under his hungry eyes and her need for more than those few seconds of his touch. There was a fleeting compulsion to reach out and pull him down for an encore, but she resisted in case it jeopardised their current non-warring status.

She let her hand fall to her side. It would be more useful lifting her discarded clothes from the floor. 'I suppose I should really pick those up,' she said, staring up at his mouth and marvelling at the way it fitted so perfectly around hers.

'Yeah,' he said, 'you really should.' Then he wrapped an arm around her waist and yanked her towards him, knocking her off her feet.

His mouth was hard on hers this time, punishing her for this inconvenient attraction, yet demanding more of her. Kayla heard a satisfied sigh escape her lips as her body melted onto his, leaving him to support them both. The flat of her hand was braced against his chest, so hard and warm beneath her finger-tips she shuddered with the solid contact. Jamie's response was to pull her closer, his hand sliding up and down the small of her back and sending darts of desire everywhere he touched.

Kayla clung to his shoulders with both hands to keep her upright as he deepened the kiss. He lashed his tongue around hers, fighting for dominance when she was happy to surrender to his will on this one occasion. Every part of her was aching with need for him, especially when she could feel his body's rock-hard confirmation he wanted her too.

'You've just had a baby,' Jamie rasped, his throat sounding as raw as hers felt holding back emotions she was afraid to unleash in the heat of his kiss.

'Your baby.' It almost seemed unbelievable now when they were just getting to know each other that she'd already borne him a child. If she'd had any hint of this passion available to her they might well have conceived the easy way.

Despite their obvious chemistry, she couldn't completely block out that ingrained instinct telling her to be wary of letting her guard down. Nothing had changed in her head simply because Jamie had kissed her; relationships were still going to be a problem for someone who had difficulty trusting a partner. The one she already had with him as Luke's father wasn't something she could afford to mess up. It was more important for her son to have a dad than it was for her to have some ill-fated affair with the nearest man available to her. Even if she wasn't still recovering from the birth, she knew this couldn't go any further.

The sound of Luke's cries from across the hall interrupted Jamie's path as he moved his lips across the edge of her jaw. He stopped just before he kissed that sweet spot behind her ear that made her knees buckle with the right man. Physically, Jamie Garrett felt very much like the right man, but no such being could possibly exist for Kayla in real life.

'I should go and feed him.' Her body was for sustaining her baby now, not feeding her need for intimacy.

Jamie took a step back, putting some much-needed distance between them. He fought to get his breathing, and the rest of his body, back under control. It wasn't easy when she was standing in front of him with kiss-swollen lips, the strap of her nightdress falling down to expose her soft, pale skin and looking thoroughly ravished.

The signs had been there for a while that something was fizzing between them. Lingering looks, that personality clash gradually turning into mutual respect, and lying in bed together watching their son sleep had all been building up to that kiss. It hadn't disappointed. That release of finally satisfying his craving was short-lived. Now he'd tasted her full lips, had her soft flesh moulded around his body, he wanted more. All of her. Walking away now was like trying to stuff a cork back into a still-fizzing bottle of champagne, yet he knew he had to. Neither her body nor her soul were ready for that. He wasn't sure he was.

After Natalie he swore he'd never lead another woman on believing there was something more to their relationship than he was willing to give. It was Kayla's strength that drew him. That stubborn streak that said she didn't need him was intoxicating to a commitment-phobe. Yet, getting involved with his son's mother would be the ultimate lifetime commitment. Something he just couldn't give.

'Give me a shout when you want me to take over.' Although Jamie didn't want her to bear the brunt of the childcare and sleepless nights, he might make an exception tonight. He needed time to process what had just happened and why he'd instigated that kiss. The spontaneous passion they'd just submitted to wasn't something easily dismissed or forgotten.

After everything she'd gone through he didn't want to betray the trust Kayla was already putting in him by letting him stay here in the house. He'd never been in the market for a family and although he now had a son, he couldn't promise her for ever. That was what it would take for a woman like Kayla, who'd been taken advantage of too often. She needed support, not someone else using her for what she could give him. Kayla wanted to be the best mother she could for Luke and he didn't want to get in the way of that.

Jamie had been doing things on his own for too long to suddenly have to share his world with someone new. He was just trying to get his head around being a father and all the responsibility and disruption that entailed. There was no way he could be a partner, a boyfriend, or whoever Kayla needed to help her move past those trust issues created by her parents.

Not when he had his own to deal with.

CHAPTER EIGHT

KAYLA YAWNED AND STRETCHED. She actually felt as though she'd had a proper night's sleep. The first since Luke had been born. A glance at the clock told her it was seven-thirty a.m. That was a lie-in as far as she was concerned. He'd slept better too, his body clock seeming to adjust since he'd taken fewer feeds through the night.

It was like waking up on a bright summer's day even though she'd yet to open the curtains. Not only was she rested but, thanks to Jamie, her dreams had been full of stolen kisses and passionate embraces. She was definitely starting the day on a high.

Even though they'd both probably come to realise they'd made a mistake, the memory of that one erotic moment would put her in a good mood for the rest of the day.

He'd been so good to her and Luke, she daredn't jeopardise that by getting carried away by one kiss. It was probably the longest he'd gone without female company of the intimate kind and he'd merely wanted to make sure fatherhood hadn't killed his pulling power. Certainly not with her anyway.

She coupled the lazy smile on her face with another stretch. Jamie must've taken Luke downstairs again so as not disturb her. Now she'd stopped searching for ulterior motives in his every action she could see how thoughtful he was.

Lying on her back, staring at the ceiling, she wondered if she was supposed to lie here until her assistance was required with the baby. Perhaps he intended to surprise her with breakfast in bed. She rolled over onto her side, ready for a second sleep when she heard fidgeting in the room, followed by a baby grizzling.

'Luke?' Sure enough when she peeked over the side of the bed into his Moses basket he was just beginning to stir. 'Time to get up, lazybones. I wonder if Daddy's slept in this morning too?'

Luke gazed up at her with familiar big eyes. 'You look just like your daddy. Don't tell him I said it, but you'll have the girls queuing up at your door when you're older.'

She scooped him up, cherishing this quiet moment, both contented to be where they were. There was only one thing missing from this family scene. 'Why don't we go and see if Daddy's up yet?'

Jamie was always keen to help bath Luke and two pairs of hands were always better than one.

'Jamie? Are you up yet?' With Luke cradled in one arm, she knocked on his bedroom door. When there was no reply she eased the door open, but the bed had already been made and the curtains opened.

'He must be downstairs. We'll sneak down and surprise him.' She rubbed Luke's nose with hers. This was what mornings were for, long lie-ins and playing with their son.

She tiptoed down the stairs, careful to avoid that one step that squeaked near the bottom and might give her away. It was starting to feel like a family home again and she couldn't wait until Luke was old enough for them to play hide and seek properly.

Suddenly, the thought of him being able to play those carefree childhood games that had been unavailable to her under her parents' roof now held so much significance. They'd hated noise. When she and Liam had been permitted to play, they'd had to do so under the threat of violence in case they were too loud. Although her brother had constantly challenged their rules and rebelled against the strict regime, Kayla had always tried to be on her best behaviour, afraid to upset them. It had taken moving to a different country to break that pattern and she didn't want another generation of her family to be tainted by messed-up parents.

Whatever happened with her and Jamie, she wanted her son to be happy, to have fun and, most of all, feel safe in his own home. There was no reason why she couldn't start doing that for him from now. Once they were fed and dressed it was time to go out and have some fun.

'Jamie, why don't we take Luke out for a walk in the pram?' She wandered into the kitchen, convinced his silence would be explained once she found him tucking into breakfast there.

Except the kitchen was empty. There wasn't as much as a dirty dish left as evidence he'd been there. She walked over and touched the kettle. It was cold. This was beginning to feel as if she were living in a mystery novel. Then she saw a note stuck to the fridge using the blue dragonfly magnet Liam had made for her out of polymer clay, holding it in place.

Didn't want to wake you two sleeping beauties!
Gone to work to catch up on some paperwork.
See you later, J

A stone dropped into Kayla's stomach. So much for her happy family day out. Jamie had sneaked back to work without a word. Not even a kiss on the note. As if last night had never happened. Perhaps that was why he'd gone this morning before she'd had a chance to see him. He regretted it.

Kayla knew anything more than being Luke's parents was probably a bad idea, but she didn't regret the kiss when it had been so amazing, so real. If it was going to change things between them she needed to know now for Luke's sake as well as her own. They couldn't provide a safe, loving home for their son if his father kept avoiding his mother over one lust-fuelled misadventure. She didn't want either of them to live with that sort of uncertainty and refused to be emotionally manipulated by anyone again, no matter how unintentional.

'Well, little man, it looks as though it's just you and me. If Daddy doesn't want to spend the day with us, it's his loss.'

'Everything looks great. You have a very strong boy here. Absolutely nothing to worry about, Mrs Hills.' Jamie put the baby's nappy back on as soon as he was able to after giving him a thorough check-over. He knew all too well what could happen when his son had christened most of his shirts during changes.

'Thanks, Doctor.' Ellie, the health visitor at the clinic, lifted the clothes they'd stripped off the baby earlier and attempted to take over.

'It's fine, I can get him dressed. I've had plenty of practice lately.' He didn't have anything else to do anyway. The staff had been shocked to see him this morning and, since there was a locum in situ in his office, he was surplus to requirements. With the baby clinic on this morning he'd volunteered his services to Ellie rather than return home.

He was being a coward, he knew it, but he'd needed to get out of that house and that world he and Kayla had built for themselves there. It wasn't real life. As demonstrated last night with his unprompted make-out session with Kayla. It didn't matter she'd apparently been holding back too, given her equally animalistic response to the kiss. This morning he'd made the decision to come into the surgery and back to some semblance of normality. He and Kayla had been living on top of each other taking care of Luke, and he was worried it was clouding his judgement. They'd become each other's world and that was possibly why they'd suddenly acted on that attraction that had been there since the wedding. Neither of them was in the right place for a serious relationship and that was the only type available to them now they were parents. A fling would make things awkward when it ended, and they still had to make decisions and time together for their son.

'Dr Garrett has just become a father himself,' Ellie explained to her patient, though she was probably just coming to terms with the news herself. He kept his personal life to himself and, although he'd had to tell the partners about his impending fatherhood, the first most people had known was when he'd gone on paternity leave. The circumstances weren't anybody's business and, to be honest, he wouldn't know where to begin explaining it. Although there was bound to be gossip, he hoped his colleagues would respect his privacy.

'Oh, congratulations.'

'Thanks.' If he'd thought coming into work today would help take his mind off those left at home, he'd been very mistaken. Even if he hadn't been cooing over babies this morning, he'd spent most of his time wondering what Kayla and Luke had been doing without him. He hated to miss a moment of his boy's life now Luke was the most important person in his life, and no longer simply a gift he'd given to Tom and Liam. Then there was the note he'd left stuck to the fridge. How long had it taken Kayla to realise he was gone and how had she reacted?

There was a chance she'd be glad to get the house to herself again, but he suspected she would be miffed at the way he'd run out on her. The adult thing would have been to talk over what had happened last night, but he wasn't ready to do that when he hadn't figured out how he felt about it himself yet. He'd enjoyed it, he'd wanted more, but the timing was appalling. If only they'd given in to temptation at the wedding they might have saved themselves all this confusion now wondering 'what if?'.

'I didn't know you were married, Doctor.' Mrs Hills's casual comment was something he knew he'd hear a lot of over the next few days until people took the hint that subject was off limits.

'I'm not.' He handed back possession of her newborn with a fake smile plastered onto his face, ignoring Ellie's look of horror that someone had dared challenge him outright. He didn't want to make anyone uncomfortable, but neither was he going to lie about his circumstances to save anyone else's blushes.

'Sorry. It's none of my business. There aren't many people who do get married these days, I suppose—'

She was frantically rocking her baby and trying to backtrack at the same time, but it was Ellie who stepped in and put an end to the awkward conversation.

'Thanks for your help, Doctor. I'm sure you have other patients to get back to.'

He didn't but it was the excuse he needed to get away from further interrogation. 'No problem. If you need me for anything else, give me a shout.'

He didn't have an office to retreat to today. It wouldn't be very professional of him to barge in and wrest control back from his substitute. Instead, he made his way to the staff room. He couldn't remember the last time he'd managed to drink a full, hot cup of coffee without interruption. Although, as he sat down in the quiet room, feet up, he couldn't help thinking about Kayla and Luke. She wouldn't have time out from parenthood and he didn't want to get used to it himself. Despite his reservations about taking on that responsibility again, he'd slipped back into that role of protector without too much hassle. The nappy changes and the feeding gave him quality bonding time with his son and those blissful moments during Luke's naptime were when he and Kayla got to chill out together.

He'd never lived with anyone other than his brother. That implied a commitment he'd never been willing to give to a woman. Yet, he and Kayla had fallen into a comfortable existence, forming a relationship neither of them had seen coming. He liked being part of a family again, enjoyed her company and loved having someone to talk to at the end of the day.

As Jamie sat alone with his cup of coffee the silence was overwhelming. Heaven help him, he was missing Kayla and his boy after only a few hours of being parted from them.

Rachel, one of the receptionists, opened the door and reminded him he wasn't so alone after all. 'Dr Garrett, your, um, your son is here to see you.'

Luke certainly hadn't come down here on his own and since the flustered member of staff didn't seem to know how to address his visitor it meant only one thing. Kayla was here too. His day was beginning to look up.

'I hear Dr Garrett is helping with the baby clinic today. That's made my day, I tell you. Very easy on the eye.'

The woman sitting beside Kayla leaned in to share her news, bouncing her curly-haired daughter on her knee. She was clearly looking forward to her appointment and as Kayla glanced around the waiting room all the other mums were chatting excitedly at the prospect too.

'I'm not here for—'

'Don't get me wrong, he's an excellent doctor, has time for everyone, but a little eye candy doesn't hurt every now and then.' Jamie's number-one fan gave her a wink as she was called next for her appointment. Kayla gave a little smile. He'd love to know he was thought of as eye candy amongst the new mums and she couldn't help but feel a swell of pride as well as being territorial. He was her baby's father and she wasn't sure how she felt about other women ogling him. Then again, as far as she knew, she was the only woman in the room he'd kissed.

She was taking a risk by coming here unannounced. Especially when he'd skipped out on her this morning without as much as a goodbye. She'd been in something of a temper when she'd left the house. One that hadn't been improved by trying to manoeuvre a pram onto a bus for the first time. Although it had to have been easier than taking the Tube. She didn't know why she'd headed to the clinic other than a need to confront Jamie about his behaviour this morning.

However, as she'd pushed Luke's pram through St James's park and seen tourists and families making the most of the summer sunshine together, she couldn't help but think he was missing out. He mightn't want to spend time with her but that didn't mean he had to lose that quality time with his son. If he wanted to take Luke for an afternoon in the park she'd happily settle for some respite at home. It wasn't as though he was scheduled to work today anyway; he was simply avoiding her. She'd had no idea he'd be taking the baby clinic, but it meant she blended in with the rest of the crowd waiting to see him. Although the receptionist had looked taken aback when she'd said his son was here.

She was waiting for someone to either call her through or throw her out when the man himself appeared in the waiting room. All the women in the room sat up a little straighter, including her.

'Kayla? Come on through.' He was smiling, looked pleased to see her. Then again, he probably wore that expression for all his patients.

Her last thought as she followed him down the corridor was how disappointed that other woman was going to be when she realised he wasn't going to be there for her appointment.

'I'm sorry to impose on you like this at work.' As she pushed Luke's pram through the clinic, seeing the other mums coming and going who actually had good reason to be here, Kayla realised how selfish she'd been turning up like this. He was a busy man, a doctor in demand, a lot of things to a lot of people, not just her.

'Don't be daft. It's good to see you.' He stopped at one of the doors lining the hall and kissed her on the cheek. Okay, it wasn't a full-on snog but at least he wasn't recoiling from her in disgust. Whatever his reason for coming in here today he did appear genuinely pleased to see them. Although, that might have more to do with the cute passenger in the pram.

'I didn't know you were going back to work. I thought you still had some holidays booked off?' If she'd had any idea it mightn't have been such a shock this morning or seemed like an excuse to put some distance between them. An idea that couldn't be totally dismissed when he ushered her into the room and closed the door as though embarrassed to be seen with her.

'It was a spur-of-the-moment decision. Now, can I get you a drink?' It was then Kayla realised he'd brought her into a communal room rather than his office.

'No, thanks. Luke and I were just out for a stroll and thought we'd pop in and say hello. I can see you're busy, though. We'll see you at home later.' She was reversing back out of the door, convinced he'd brought her in here because he thought there'd be safety in numbers once those extra chairs in the room were filled with other members of staff.

'Don't go. Honestly, I think I'm just in the way here today. Why don't I come with you? Where were you headed?' This turnaround was making her head spin, wondering what could have happened in the few hours since he'd left the house that he actually wanted to spend time with them now.

'We were going to go to the park, maybe go and see the ducks. It's nice outside. I thought we'd make the most of the good weather.' She hadn't planned much beyond calling in to see what had driven him out first thing this morning. Whatever the cause, it seemed to have passed now otherwise he wouldn't be so keen to join them outside in the real world.

'Sounds good. Let me tell them I'm leaving for the day and I'll join you. Have you eaten?'

'We had some breakfast when we woke up, but I guess it'll be lunch time soon. I'm sure Luke will let me know when he's hungry.'

'Why don't we stop and get some food to take with us to the park, then we can really make the most of the afternoon?'

'Sure.' It was an unexpected turn of events but certainly one Kayla wasn't going to turn down. Spending the day kicking back with Jamie and Luke in the park sounded like the tonic she needed.

* * *

There was none of that macho nonsense preventing Jamie from being seen pushing a pram. If anything, Kayla thought she might have to wrest it from him to get her turn. He wheeled Luke through the clinic, pride exuding from every pore as he introduced his son to every person who stopped him to take a peek.

She didn't miss the curious looks directed at her from waiting patients and in a fit of pique made sure her hand rested possessively on the handle too. This was her family. Regardless of what did or didn't happen between her and Jamie, they were Luke's parents. Jamie was always going to be his dad and part of her life.

'He's quite the crowd-puller,' Jamie boasted, striding out onto the street, smiling at every passerby. Kayla wasn't going to fuel his ego by pointing out a handsome, eligible doctor with a baby was the main attraction.

'We should get you a puppy, then you'd have the attention of every female, and quite a few males, within a hundred-mile radius.' His failure to introduce her as anyone significant to his admirers prompted an uncharacteristic pang of sadness. It hadn't done anything to quell her fear she was still playing the role of surrogate. The oven for Jamie's bun, which he wanted to share with everyone but her.

He frowned at her, the barb not hitting home. 'I'd never get any work done. Listen, there's a place on the corner that does a nice lunch selection. Why don't you take over here and I'll grab us some takeout?'

'I'd be honoured.' So far, the most she'd been permitted to do was adjust the parasol attached to the pram to prevent the sun from shining in on Luke.

It wasn't that she was jealous of the attention Jamie was giving Luke, or that she was being edged out so Daddy could take over. No, her sudden bout of petulant behaviour had come about because it was clear they were no longer acting as a cohesive couple out in public. Despite everything telling her it wasn't possible, she wanted them to be a team, to be together. When he'd agreed to leave work and come with them he'd given her that fizz of hope in her belly that there was a chance last night's passionate embrace hadn't been a one-off after all.

He met her back out on the pavement holding up a paper bag in triumph. The sort that said the deli catered for exclusive diets and tastes rather than some nondescript takeaway that served up cold pasties and sandwiches to the masses.

'That's lunch sorted. Now to find somewhere to eat it.' He was so utterly charming and thoughtful it was hard to remain mad at him for long.

He wasn't organising a picnic in the park for Luke's benefit, or to keep his adoring fan club happy. This was entirely for her and him. An afternoon relaxing in the sun like any other couple. Those clouds that had been steadily moving in to spoil her day began to dissipate until her smile was as bright as the sun shining overhead.

They walked on through the park, past families playing ball games, couples stretched out together on the green and dog walkers trying to get their enthusiastic charges under control.

'How about here?' Jamie found a shady spot beneath a huge tree, far enough from the sun worshippers to provide privacy whilst she fed Luke.

'Perfect.' She put the brakes on the pram, and Jamie stripped off his jacket to spread it out on the grass.

'There's really no need to ruin your suit on my account.' Although she appreciated the gesture, she could only imagine the cost of getting grass stains out of the expensive light grey fabric.

'I can't have the mother of my child sitting on wet grass, can I? I'm a gentleman. Now, take a seat and I'll serve lunch.' From anyone else Kayla would've judged the gesture over the top, but she'd seen sufficient similar behaviour to know he was the genuine article.

She lifted Luke out and sat down to feed him with the thick tree trunk providing excellent support for her back. The tangle of branches above their heads also shielded them from the glare of the afternoon sun.

Jamie lay down beside her, putting the other half of his suit at risk by lying on the grass. He kicked off his shoes and socks, removed his tie and loosened his collar. 'That's better.'

Kayla watched him with amusement at how quickly he'd been able to switch off from work and relax. 'Why don't you make yourself comfortable?'

'If I was going to do that, the shirt and trousers would be off too, and I'd be lying here in just my boxers.' His flirty wink coupled with an image she'd got to know well around the house conspired to raise her temperature so much she might as well have been sitting in direct sunlight.

'Well, we don't want to have to bail Daddy out of jail so I'd advise keeping your clothes on for now.' Kayla adjusted her blouse once Luke had taken his fill, then winded him over her shoulder.

'In that case we should concentrate on filling our bellies. Especially since you have to keep your energy levels up for greedy guts here. I'll take him, and you help yourself.' They did the baby handover so Jamie was in charge of the back rubbing, leaving Kayla the pick of the deli cartons spread out on his jacket.

With the plastic cutlery provided she helped herself to some of the giant couscous jewelled with pomegranate seeds and edamame beans. The tomato and basil pasta salad filled her up quickly so she passed when Jamie offered her a share of his samosa veggie wheat wrap. Bless him, she knew he'd much rather have been tucking into a dirty big burger, but he'd gone out of his way to make this special for her. She washed her lunch down with a mouthful of pure orange juice and flopped back down on the ground.

'I'm stuffed.' That satisfying full feeling in her belly made her want to close her eyes and sleep for a while. She was content lying here with Jamie and Luke in a way she hadn't been for years, if ever.

'I wish I could say the same.' Jamie tossed the empty wrapper from his lunch back into the bag, not looking quite so gratified with his food choice.

'I'm sure there's something else left in the

bag.' She dug in again and retrieved a package of apple wedges and toffee dipping sauce for him. 'Someone's got a sweet tooth.'

'I thought we needed something decadent.' He tried to pull off the cellophane, but it wasn't easy when he was cradling Luke in one arm.

'I'll do it,' she said, opening the package and dipping an apple into the sweet, sticky sauce to hold out for him.

He dipped his head, his lips brushing against her fingers as he took the fruit from her. She watched him with fascination as he crunched on the apple. There shouldn't have been anything erotic in the act, especially given their location. Yet, she found it incredibly so, imagining that mouth accepting her as easily as the piece of apple. His tongue licking her sweetness as thoroughly as he cleaned the toffee left on her fingers, sucking each one slowly and deliberately. The whole time he was seducing her with his mouth, his eyes didn't leave hers and she knew he was imagining the same scene playing out in the bedroom. Minus the food and the audience.

'Jamie—' Her throat was as dry as other parts of her were wet.

She was unable to explore what either meant or if he was experiencing the same inner turmoil as the moment was brought to an abrupt halt by a football landing with a direct hit onto their picnic. Leftover couscous and pasta spilled out and sounded the death knell for Jamie's jacket. Luke, who had been in the land of nod, was startled awake by the noise and let out a yell. Jamie was no longer teasing her but on his feet, swearing under his breath. Her peace and contentment had come to an end.

'Sorry.' A red-faced teenage boy appeared, took one look at the mess, grabbed his ball back and ran off towards his mates.

'Be more careful next time,' she yelled after him, aware they could have hit the baby. If she'd been paying more attention to their surroundings rather than fantasising about the father of her child, she might have seen the danger headed their way. She scooped up the devastation left behind and threw it back in the bag with unnecessary force.

'Hey, no harm done.' Jamie reached out a hand to rub the small of her back, soothing her and Luke at the same time. He had that knack of knowing what was worrying her and doing what he could to defuse the tension trying to strangle those moments of serenity. On this occasion she had a right to be annoyed but sometimes uneasiness crept in uninvited at times when she let herself enjoy life. It was a hangover from those days under her parents' rule, waiting for her punishment to be dished out for forgetting her place. Which, according to them, wasn't to feel a second of happiness. Liam, and now Jamie, were the only people ever capable of blocking out those memories to live in the moment.

Like now, when he was reassuring her there was no lasting damage except to his clothes. Once again providing a calming presence for her, preventing her from spiralling into a 'what if?' scenario that would've kept her on edge for the rest of the night. She took several deep breaths to restore her pulse to its normal rhythm, then Jamie, seeming to sense her need for a cuddle, placed Luke back in her arms. Inhaling the clean, fresh scent of baby powder immersed her back into that world of innocence and a life untouched by cruelty. Her baby deserved better than a parent who couldn't move on from the past when there was so much to appreciate today.

'We're supposed to be relaxing, so come on.' Jamie sprawled out on the grass again and patted the space beside him. She accepted his invitation, placed Luke on the jacket between them, and lay down. Eyes closed, calm restored, it wasn't long before she drifted off into a peaceful slumber.

The sound of chattering children somewhere nearby filtered into Kayla's consciousness and she opened her eyes to check on Luke. There was a slight panic when she found the space next to her empty, but her eyes caught sight of Jamie sleeping nearby, with the baby lying soundly on his chest.

Her heart grew twice its size to accommodate the amount of love she had for the sight of this hunky doctor with their tiny son sleeping in the dappled sunlight. That iconic bond really ought to have been captured, in black and white, to capture the hearts of teenage girls all around the world.

She hadn't heard Luke grizzling but she supposed Jamie had moved him so as not to disturb her. Kayla rolled over onto her side to study his profile up close without that fear of being caught staring at him. There were copper threads woven through his dark, wavy hair she hadn't noticed before. The long dark lashes were a particular feature she liked, framing his beautiful brown eyes, hidden from view for now. He had a strong, straight nose, pointing like an arrow to those full lips she'd dreamed about too often.

Embracing her current live-in-the-moment mantra, she gave into impulse, leaned over and kissed him. The soft caress of his lips against hers was everything she remembered from the last time they'd touched. Then he kissed her back and blew her whole world apart once more.

Jamie was only half sleeping, enjoying the quiet and simply spending time with his favourite people in the world. When he felt that exquisite pressure on his lips he knew it was Kayla by the lemony scent of her hair falling around his face as she kissed him. This was everything he'd been waiting for and he responded with the full strength of his feelings for her with every fibre of his being.

He turned into the kiss, keeping one hand on Luke so he didn't disturb him, sliding the other into Kayla's hair to hold her where he wanted her. Her tentative tongue sought his, but Jamie was no longer holding back, increasing the intensity of the tryst with every taste of her. His mouth was hard against hers now, the rest of his body following suit, and when she moaned against his lips he knew he had to cool it or risk making a public spectacle in the park.

He pulled back, released her from his grasp and opened his eyes. Her heavy-lidded eyes, mussed hair and bruised lips suggested they'd had more than a smooch. It certainly felt like it. His heart was thudding so hard, his breathing laboured, it was no wonder Luke was beginning to stir.

'Wow. Where did that come from?' She pressed her forehead to his, her breathing coming in short gasps.

'You started it,' he said with a laugh, doing his best to lighten the crackling tension between them.

Kayla let out a long, dreamy sigh and shuffled over beside him. That unspoken question about what they did next tried to wriggle in between them, but Jamie refused to let it have room. Not when Kayla was lying with her head tucked under his arm and his son was sleeping on his chest. He didn't want anything as brutal as real life crashing in and ruining this perfect family picture.

CHAPTER NINE

NO MATTER HOW much she wanted to, Kayla knew she couldn't spend all day here lying curled up against Jamie, revelling in his solid warmth and smooching like teenagers. There was a nip in the air now that the afternoon sun was beginning to fade, and she wouldn't wish for Luke to catch a cold.

'We should put him back in his pram,' she whispered, although not keen to break the spell keeping them in this lovely daydream together.

'Just. One. More. Kiss.' He peppered her lips with tempting little pecks before drawing her bottom lip into his mouth and teasing her with the tip of his tongue. She literally could do this all day.

Luke started to grizzle and reminded her why she couldn't. Reluctantly, she drew away from Jamie's mind-bending kisses and transferred her attention back to her son. She didn't know how today's progress in their relationship was going to affect them once they were back in more familiar surroundings, but they'd have to face reality sooner or later.

'When you're older we'll be able to play football and feed the ducks like everyone else,' she told Luke as she carried him over to his pram.

'Or, you know, we could give him a brother and sister to keep him occupied while Mummy and Daddy get to kiss in peace.' Jamie rested his hand at the base of her neck as he whispered into her ear, sending her body haywire at both points of contact. She knew he was only joking. One snogging session didn't constitute a marriage proposal and two point four children. Even if they had conceived a child before their first kiss.

'You're only saying that now because we haven't been through the teething stage, potty training, the terrible twos...' Today had been blissful but she wasn't so naïve as to think every day was going to be as easy. They hadn't really been tested yet as parents, never mind as a couple. She hoped that was what they were becoming—she wasn't into kissing men on a whim. With Jamie being the father of her child and her temporary housemate, it was always going to be more complicated than just a kiss here and there. That was why she'd held back for as long as she had despite her growing feelings towards Jamie. Now she'd made that leap of faith in showing him, in trusting him, it was all or nothing for her from now on.

'All things I'm very much looking forward to.' He squeezed her close, making her heart give a giddy skip as a future together flashed before her eyes. One that wasn't as unappealing as it had once seemed.

If things carried on much the way they had been between her and Jamie she couldn't see any reason to be afraid of sharing her life with him. He'd been respectful of her need for independence, yet had helped when she'd needed it, and he was a great dad. As well as a fantastic kisser. She stopped before her imagination conjured images of other things he would be equally skilled in. Some things were worth waiting for and it would be a while before she'd be ready for anything more than they'd shared today.

A matter of weeks ago she'd been adamant she wouldn't let him invade her life or be a part of Luke's. Now as they walked home together she wanted so much more. If she was risking her heart and her whole world to let him in, this had better mean something special to him too.

'Oh, isn't he gorgeous?' Their journey home was brought to a halt by an admiring stranger. If she hadn't been leaning into the pram cooing over Luke the compliment could've been referring to either male currently in Kayla's company.

'Thank you.' She accepted the compliment on their behalf from the middle-aged woman who was now taking a keen interest in Jamie too.

'I'm about to become a grandmother for the first time soon. That's my daughter over there. Ready to pop in a couple of weeks.' The proud gran-to-be pointed to the heavily pregnant woman sitting on a park bench nearby, who gave a weak wave back.

'Is she okay?' It was Jamie who enquired after her health, though it was obvious to Kayla too the woman didn't look well at all. Her face was pale, and she was rubbing the base of her spine with both hands.

'Either she has overdone the walking, or the heat has got to her. I thought she should rest for a while before we head home again.'

Kayla steered the pram over towards the bench. She couldn't in good conscience keep on walking past a pregnant woman in discomfort, and she was sure Jamie wouldn't either. 'Hi. Your mum said you weren't feeling too well. Is there anything we can do for you?'

'I'm fine, thanks. Just some back ache. I'm sure it'll pass.' She offered a strained smile, which wasn't totally convincing.

'There's some water in the bag if you'd like a drink.' Jamie reached into the tray under the pram and pulled out a bottle.

'That would be great. I am a little dehydrated.' She accepted his help much easier and the smile shone a tad brighter as Jamie took a seat beside her on the bench.

'Would you like us to call an ambulance for you?' Kayla pulled out her mobile phone. Dr Garrett's charm, effective as it seemed now, couldn't cure whatever ailed her.

'I don't think that's necessary. I'll be all right in a minute.' She took another swig of water from the bottle.

'I'm a doctor over at the clinic. If you think you could make it that far I could give you a check-over?' Apparently Jamie wasn't going to take her word for it either and Kayla would be happier if they could get her into some sort of medical facility to check on her and the baby.

'Erin, that's not a bad idea, love. Let the doctor see what's what with you and the bub, then we can phone Gary to come and pick us up.' Her mum was kneeling down beside her now, trying to convince her to accept the offer of help.

'A midwife will be able to take a look in case you are in the early stages of labour.' Kayla understood the need to maintain her independence and some control over her body. As she'd found out for herself, it wasn't always wise to be stubborn for the sake of it this late in a pregnancy.

That seemed to jolt Erin into a reality check. 'I can walk. I haven't had any contractions and my waters haven't broken but, goodness knows, I don't want to have my baby in the middle of a public park.'

With assistance from Jamie and her mother, Erin heaved herself up from the bench.

'We can take it slow and you can hold onto the pram for support if you need it.' Kayla relinquished sole command of the pram to make room for her. It was the least she could do in the circumstances.

Once they made it to the clinic Jamie commandeered one of the cubicles in the treatment room for Erin. 'I'll go and see if the midwife is available to see you.'

He rushed off, leaving Erin and her mother in the room and Kayla uncertain of her place in the doorway with the pram. This wasn't the end to the afternoon they'd planned. Whilst she wanted to provide Erin with all the help she needed, she couldn't simply abandon her son in the process.

'Ow.' Erin's face was full of pain as she gripped her belly with both hands. 'My bump is very tight, as though it's being squeezed.'

'You may be in the early stages of labour. Hopefully the midwife can tell you for sure once she gets here.' Erin squirmed in the chair and her mother tried to get her to focus on something other than the pain.

'You're in the best place, love. Isn't it lovely in here? Looks very modern. We might have to think about changing our GP to this nice young doctor.'

A sudden gush of liquid confirmed Kayla's suspicions that Erin was in labour despite her denial.

Since Luke was sleeping soundly, Kayla ventured into the confined room. 'Don't worry, I'm sure we can get someone to clean that up. If you're in labour, you might be more comfortable up on the bed. I'll give you a hand.'

Between them, the women helped Erin onto the bed. She was still clutching her belly, her face scrunched up in pain. This contraction was intense and not letting up. Hopefully the midwife wouldn't mind Kayla getting involved. She wouldn't want to tread on anyone's toes professionally, but she wanted Erin to remain as calm as possible. A first baby was special, and the memory of the birth lasted a lifetime. If she was going to be part of it, she wanted to be sure she'd done everything in her power to make it as painless as possible for the mother.

'Okay, the bad news is the midwife and health visitor are out on their rounds. The good news is that Kayla here is a qualified midwife.' Jamie rushed back to land her right in the middle of the unfolding drama.

'Erin's waters have just broken. You're going to have to call an ambulance. I don't practise any more, remember? I'm a doula now. I support patients more on an emotional basis these days, Erin.' She wanted to be transparent about her professional limitations since she'd left the hospital. Then it was down to Erin whether or not she wanted her to be involved.

'She practically delivered our baby herself.' Of course, Jamie was singing her praises, because it would get him off the hook. He'd already helped deliver one unexpected surprise and clearly wasn't in a hurry to do it again.

'Not exactly,' she tried to protest when he'd done as much to bring Luke safely into the world.

'I just want someone to tell me everything's all right,' Erin cried out. In pregnancy, the unknown simply increased anxiety levels at an already stressful time.

'I'm sure it is. I merely want to make sure everyone's on board with me doing the checks?' Everyone nodded enthusiastically. 'What about Luke?'

'My secretary is on her way to babysit. I'm sure we'll have the whole staff vying for cuddles. He'll be fine.'

With no more excuses available, Kayla went to the wash station to scrub up before she did an examination.

'Dr Garrett, I'd like you to be present too so you can report I've followed all relevant procedures.' He could also provide medical backup if needed. It was his practice after all. She'd only come in to invite him out for lunch.

'I'm going to phone for that ambulance and let the rest of the staff know what's happening in here.'

'There's a real pressure pushing down. It feels weird down there and it hurts real bad.'

'In that case, Erin, I'm going to have to do an internal exam. Is that okay?' As soon as she was given permission she covered Erin's lower half with a modesty sheet and helped her remove her underclothes.

The problem was immediately obvious. 'Okay, Erin. You're fully dilated. I can already see the head.'

Jamie returned as she delivered the news and seemed to realise this baby wasn't hanging on for the ambulance, rushing around to get the necessary equipment organised for the impending birth.

'That's not possible. I'm having my baby in hospital. Gary's going to be with me. I don't have the music I picked out or my delivery bag with me.'

'I know, but Junior is in a hurry to meet his mummy. This time tomorrow you could be sitting at home with him.' Kayla knew it was a shock. Precipitate labour, or fast labour, didn't give any thought to the nine months the mother had spent planning how her delivery and birth would go.

It was difficult for those mums to adjust to labour and develop a coping strategy when the contractions could involve one long, intense, continuous pain. The important thing was to make sure the baby was delivered safely when there were dangers involved in such rapid births. At least she was in a clinic with medical professionals and hadn't given birth in a public toilet in the park.

There was no time for pain relief or even a need to cut Erin as her son slid out after just a couple of pushes.

Kayla's elation and relief evaporated quickly when she saw the green tinge to the baby's skin. He was having difficulty breathing and his little body was limp. 'I think he's inhaled the meconium.'

'Give him to me. I need an endotracheal

tube,' Jamie yelled to the nurses and staff assembled outside the cubicle as the drama unfolded.

Meconium, baby's first faeces passed in the womb, could become trapped in the baby's airways or lungs if inhaled. The severity of meconium aspiration, dependent on the amount inhaled, could lead to long-term complications including lung problems, hearing loss or neurological damage. In some rarer cases it could even lead to death. It was vital they got him breathing.

'What is it? What's wrong with my baby?' Erin was sobbing and clutching her mother's hand as Kayla passed him to Jamie.

She knew that heart-stopping fear of thinking something terrible was threatening your baby's life having gone through it only days ago herself. Although Kayla would want her to know what was happening it was as important to keep her calm as it was to keep her informed.

'He's having a little trouble breathing. We need to clear his airways as much as we can. The ambulance will be here any second. I'm sure the hospital staff are on standby to make sure you get the treatment you need straight away.' He might need to go into a neonatal intensive care unit to be closely watched, but he'd receive antibiotics and oxygen therapy to help him on the road to recovery.

Jamie inserted the flexible plastic tube into the baby's windpipe through his mouth to suction his airways. He continued clearing until there were no visible signs of the meconium in the suctioned fluids, working so calmly and efficiently one would have thought this was his area of expertise.

The paramedics arrived then and took over, administering oxygen as they ushered mother and baby to the waiting ambulance. Kayla and Jamie exchanged relieved smiles across the room strewn with debris from the emergency delivery that had thankfully ended well.

They made a good team. Twice now they'd worked together through possible birth complications. It made her think about the future and the possibilities out there for the two of them. Especially now when she was reminded how much good she could still do as a midwife helping to bring children into the world.

'Oh, you like that, don't you?' As Jamie held his slippery son still in the bath, Kayla scooped water over his scalp and body to rinse off the soap suds. Bath time was fast becoming a highlight as they spent this quality time together with Luke.

'It won't be long before we're reading him bedtime stories too.' There wasn't a sound out of Luke except for contented gurgling as Kayla lifted him out to wrap him in a fluffy towel.

It was a domestic scene he'd never imagined he'd be part of again. Yet it was a much-needed slice of normal life after the fraught afternoon. He imagined it would be the same after a full day treating his patients at the clinic. Something worth coming home for.

'I'll look forward to that. I know I was only supposed to be staying in the interim, but I'd like to be around to do more of this kind of stuff.' He'd resisted the idea of family until he'd nearly lost it all. Thanks to Kayla and Luke, this was a chance to be part of one again. To belong somewhere other than work was as though a whole new world was opening up to him.

'Sure. We don't have to put anything formal in place. I think we're doing okay the way we are.' She kissed him full on the lips as she passed him on the way to the bedroom, but it didn't put his mind fully to rest.

They might have made roads towards a relationship, but it was early days. He wasn't expecting any commitment there yet, but he was keen to know where he stood in terms of being Luke's father.

Once the baby was settled into his night's sleep Jamie dropped a gentle kiss on his forehead. 'Goodnight, son.'

Being able to do that, to say those words, brought a lump to his throat. With every passing day as a dad he found it more difficult to understand his own father's behaviour. Family life had never been enough for him. Whereas Jamie found pleasure in every moment with his son and wouldn't voluntarily be deprived of a second of it. Sorrow balled in his gut too when he remembered how much his brother had wanted this baby and would never get to experience the joy of fatherhood for himself. It was something Jamie would never take for granted when he knew how privileged he was to have been given this gift.

Today had been a reminder of how precious, and fragile, life was. Neither he, nor Kayla, had been able to save their brothers but if they could prevent one more unnecessary death all the training and hard work had been worth it.

'I wish Tom and Liam could have been here to see this,' he said, uncharacteristically sentimental as he watched his sleeping son.

'Me too,' Kayla said before giving him a much-needed hug.

When she let go, much too quickly for his liking, she went to check the baby monitor was switched on and gave their son one last kiss. "Night, sweetheart.'

Once they'd tiptoed out of the room and closed the door she let out a long sigh as though she was finally allowing herself to relax.

'Come on. I think we're due some down time.' Jamie took her hand and led her down to the living room, sat her down on the sofa and took off her shoes. He kicked off his own before lying lengthways on the settee, bringing her with him so she was lying in his arms.

'This is nice,' she mumbled and snuggled into him. It didn't matter to Jamie how cramped it was with both of them lying here when her body was packed so pleasantly against his.

'We had a busy day. It's nice to be able to come home and do this.' If he had his way he'd be able to do it every day. He didn't want to rush her, but he didn't see the point in wasting time. They wanted to be with each other, to be there for their son.

Tom and Liam's accident had shown him he shouldn't take anything for granted and he wanted to be the best partner for Kayla, the greatest dad to Luke. He believed the best way to achieve that was by moving in with them permanently.

'I'll admit, it wasn't the return to work I'd planned.' She rotated her position until she was face to face with him.

'No, but I'm glad you were there.'

'Likewise.'

'You were great putting Erin's mind at ease that we knew what we were doing, and the baby was going to be all right. It's impressive watching you work.'

She batted his shoulder, deflecting the compliment when he'd been the one who'd saved the baby's life. 'You're just saying that because you think I'm the type of girl who'll swoon if a doctor praises her.'

'And you're not?' He leaned in closer, his eyes trained on her lips as he locked onto his target.

'It depends on the doctor.'

'Kayla, I want you to know I will never tell you something simply because I think it's what you want to hear. I'll always be honest with you.' He couldn't imagine ever feeling the need to lie to Kayla when it was the one thing guaranteed to lose her for ever now she'd started to trust him. After everything she'd been through he was privileged even to be with her here. A position he was not about to abuse.

'I think that's the nicest thing anyone has ever said to me.' She looked up at him, the teasing putting a twinkle in her eye and tilting her lips up towards him.

'Uh-huh. Well, here's another one for you. I've never been as happy as I have been with you and Luke these past days.' Despite her attempts to lighten the mood he wanted her to know he was serious in his commitment.

Jamie understood her need to protect herself and Luke. By swearing off long-term relationships he'd erected those same barriers around his heart. Yet there was no denying they were beginning to crumble. He'd fallen for Kayla and that wasn't going to change simply because he was afraid of being tied down again. That had happened the moment he'd decided to step up and be the father his son needed. If anything, that should have made him warier of getting into a relationship with Luke's mother.

Her eyes misted with tears and he watched

her throat bob as she swallowed them back. 'Shut up and kiss me.'

He smiled at her directness and knew it was her way of telling him she felt the same without saying the words. If she didn't reciprocate the sentiment she would've told him rather than force either of them to live a lie.

It was nice to be with someone who told it as it was instead of leaving him to guess what she wanted from him. Kayla was a strong, decisive woman who wouldn't put up with any nonsense or be wishy-washy about being with him. She was an all-or-nothing girl, which suited him because he wanted everything she had to give.

He took possession of her mouth with his, her body sighing against him as they joined together. With his hand splayed on her lower back under her shirt, she quivered at his touch. In turn, she rested her hand on his chest, his heart trying to burst free at the simple contact.

With every kiss, every caress of her lips, his body grew harder, wanting more, yet he was content with what they had here. A kiss between two single adults shouldn't be a big deal, but in some ways it was everything. Jamie had enjoyed one-night stands in the past to relieve sexual tension, but somehow this seemed more intimate. Sex could mean nothing other than a physical release at times, but lying here, kissing the mother of his baby, was a whole new ball game.

They hadn't even taken their clothes off yet and he was picturing their future together as a family. He intended to take things slowly with Kayla from here on in so he didn't ruin things. Something told him once they consummated this relationship it would be for ever. The timing had to be perfect and they had to be together for the right reasons. Not simply down to convenience or confused emotions. He didn't want to ruin what they had, or what they could have, together.

Slowly, frustratingly, he eased back on the intensity of the kiss. Kayla too seemed to realise they couldn't carry on without burning each other out with this sudden flare of passion. She huffed out another sigh and rested her head on his chest.

He stroked her hair until her eyes fluttered shut and her breathing was deep and even. She was exhausted. He was too, trying to work through these new emotions. One thing was for sure. He'd rather be here, wide awake with Kayla in his arms, than go to bed alone. That single life he'd wanted for so long was now a thing of the past. Everything he wanted was right here.

CHAPTER TEN

'I'LL BE HOME as soon as I can get away.' Jamie leaned over the sofa and gave Kayla a peck on the lips.

They'd fallen asleep here last night and he'd almost slept in. Luke too had chosen to have a lie-in this morning. With two of them squashed onto the settee it should've been the most uncomfortable sleep ever, but it had been quite the opposite. Wrapped up in Jamie, she'd had the best slumber she'd had in a long time. Now Jamie was referring to the place as home she was hoping it was the first of many nights together to come.

'Good. I'll be here, waiting.' Not right here, she had to get washed and dressed and sort Luke out, but she would be looking forward to Jamie's return. His kisses were worth hanging around for. He made her feel free again, liberated from her hang-ups. She'd trusted him and, so far, he was doing everything right. He wasn't even pressuring her for more than a kiss and a cuddle when it was evident they both wanted more. Instead of leaving for work, Jamie bent down again to kiss her more thoroughly. Then he deliberately toppled over the couch, careful not to hurt her as he covered her with his body. Her giggling was halted as he kissed her longer and deeper.

'As much as I could do this all day, one of us has work to go to.' If they did much more canoodling they'd end up going further than she was ready for physically or mentally. She didn't want to rush into anything. Since they were already living together and had a child, she thought they could take their time with the physical side of the relationship. She could do without the pressure on her to be anyone but herself. There'd been too much of her life spent being Kayla the perfect daughter, the grieving sister, and overwhelmed mum. She didn't want to dive right into being Kayla the girlfriend and losing her identity all over again. It would be nice just to be herself and not worrying if that was enough.

Jamie groaned and, with one last hard smooch, climbed off her again.

'Later,' he said, his voice huskier than she'd ever heard and sending her insides into raptures. That promise of an extended couch cuddle gave her shivers. When one word and a few kisses had become the most erotic moment of her life, she knew she was investing too much into one man. Her imagination and libido were running away with thoughts about the effect the next stage of their relationship could have on her, but at what cost?

There were more than her feelings to consider. She had a son now. If it all went wrong, and she lost herself again, she couldn't simply start over the way she had the last time. Liam wasn't here to pick her up and put her back together and, as Luke's father, Jamie was always going to be a part of her life. He'd told her his relationship history and hadn't made any promises that he could commit to her any more than he had to any other woman. She had to ask herself if the growing feelings she had for him were worth acting on after all, if heartbreak was inevitable.

'You've had a busy few days, then?' Cherry sat down with two mugs of herbal tea. Although a visitor in the house on this occasion, she'd made the tea, leaving Kayla free to nurse Luke.

She'd filled her in on the events at Jamie's clinic after their walk in the park. Neglecting to share the developments between them on a romantic level.

'Yes. I'd forgotten what that adrenaline rush was like to be involved in those emergency cases. It's so good knowing you've helped a mother and baby during difficult times.' Her role recently had become sedate, more of a counselling basis than being an active participant in the birth. Whilst rewarding in itself, her involvement yesterday had her thinking about where she would do the most good.

The speed with which her relationship with Jamie was moving had also given her pause for thought. She was beginning to think she needed some space from him before things progressed any further.

'Sounds to me as though someone's missing work.' Cherry eyed her over the cup as she sipped, knowing Kayla wasn't one to sit still for long. She might have struggled with motherhood initially but now she was thinking about getting the rest of her life back on track too.

'It's more than that. In some ways, now that I'm a mother myself I want to do something for those who aren't as fortunate as I've been. I mean, I had you and Jamie to support me during a relatively straightforward birth. There are so many people I could help with my qualifications and experience.' Yesterday had given her a taste of what could be achieved if she was in the right place at the right time. Although she was savouring the wonders of motherhood, she couldn't, and didn't want to be at home for ever. There was a big world outside Jamie Garrett and she'd do well to remember that.

Since leaving home she'd always worked to support herself, not relying on anyone else and she wasn't about to start now. Sharing a house and a child with Jamie didn't mean she was going to hand over control of her life in a package with her heart.

'What are you thinking about? Are there big changes afoot?' As ever, she could count on Cherry being supportive, never being critical, or telling her what she should do. In these circumstances she knew her parents would insist she stayed at home devoted to her baby. Hypocritical, but that was who they were. They would never have admitted to being bad parents, only of having bad children.

Mind you, they would have keeled over at the notion of her being an unmarried mother shacked up with the man who got her pregnant. The thought did secretly make her smile and she imagined telling them the circumstances behind Luke's birth to see the looks on their faces. The sort of thing Liam would've done purely to spite their tyrannical doctrine. Except Luke was hers and they had absolutely no right to taint him with their vile ways.

'It did get me thinking about Liam and

Tom's project in Vietnam. They worked so hard to fund that community and set up a clinic there. I wondered about going out there to help for a while and get a real idea of what they achieved.' It would bring her closer to them and she could even visit their graves and say her goodbyes properly. She knew they would've approved her plans. Even more so if she brought Luke with her to be a part of it all.

'I'm sure there would always be a need for qualified medical staff. Have you thought about what you would do with Buster, here?' Cherry lifted the end of Luke's bib to wipe away some of the milk he'd brought up when he'd been winded.

'I don't think there'd be a problem taking him with me. I'd still be feeding him myself, so it makes sense.' It wouldn't be a normal working environment where it would be frowned upon to bring her baby with her. Besides, it would encourage other mothers to see him there and realise she knew what she was doing.

'What does Jamie think about that?' It was

Cherry's not so subtle way of reminding her there were two parents to consider but she wasn't about to abscond with their baby for ever.

'I haven't told him yet.' Seeing Cherry's raised eyebrow, she added, 'I'm going to tell him tonight.'

'Uh huh. You let me know how that goes.'

'What do you mean?' Kayla found herself getting defensive at Cherry's sarcastic tone.

'I mean, Jamie doesn't strike me as the kind of dad who'll sit back and let you take his son halfway around the world without a say.'

There was that word *let* again. Why did everyone think she needed permission to run her own life?

'Maybe you don't know him the way I do.'

'Yes, I doubt I do. The glow about you these days has nothing to do with post-pregnancy hormones and everything, I suspect, to do with your new housemate.' If Cherry was trying to avoid an argument and fish for gossip at the same time, she'd hooked herself a whopper.

There was no way Kayla could keep her

secret for ever. 'Things have…evolved over these past days.'

'I knew it!' Eyes wide, mouth open, Cherry leaned in, waiting for her to spill the details.

'We've only kissed but I think it could lead to something more serious.' They hadn't discussed what they wanted to come from this new development, but neither of them would want to jeopardise Luke's future for a mere fling.

'That's great. I'm so happy for you and I'm sure Liam and Tom would be too.' The touch of Cherry's hand on hers and the reminder of her brother brought tears to Kayla's eyes.

This situation would've appealed to Liam's warped sense of humour and Tom's romantic nature. They would've taken credit for the matchmaking too. If not for them or Luke, she would never have realised what a great man Jamie was or how great a father he'd make. Except she wanted to take his son, his only family, to the very place that had claimed his brother's life to escape her feelings for him.

'I wouldn't start celebrating just yet. I don't

think I'm ready to get into a relationship with someone who has made it very clear he doesn't do commitment. He hasn't even suggested moving in permanently, for goodness' sake.' If he'd shown her any sign she meant anything more than Natalie, or his other past conquests, she might have considered it worth the risk of making a go of things. There was too much to lose based on a case of wishful thinking.

'Don't write him off altogether. Talk things over first. I know you've been hurt in the past, but this could be the start of a great future together for the two of you.'

'I wish I could believe that, Cherry.' She sighed, but life had taught her not to expect too much. That was exactly what it would be if she believed Jamie would commit to her for ever. Too much.

More than ever, Jamie was grateful he'd gone into general medicine rather than the frantic pace of emergency care. Life as a doctor would never run to nine to five, Monday to Friday shifts, but he did have some down time when he wasn't on call. In hindsight he shouldn't have been in such a rush to get back to work and made the most of his paternity leave to squeeze out every second of quality time with his family. It was too late now. He'd made the knee-jerk decision to go back simply because he'd feared getting too close. Now he realised home with his family was where he wanted to be more than anywhere else.

Perhaps it had taken that short separation for him to realise that. It could've been spending that afternoon with them that reminded him of the important things in his life. Whatever it was that had changed his views from the pitfalls of domesticity to the rewards of having people he cared about around him, there was something to look forward to at the end of every shift.

He used his key to let himself into the house, careful not to make too much noise in case Luke was sleeping and he woke him up.

'Hey,' he said softly as Kayla peeped her head around the doorframe.

'Dinner's ready,' she said with a grin.

'Now that's what I call a welcome home.' He could get used to this. Especially if he came home to Kayla's kisses and a home-cooked meal every night. He couldn't remember the last time anyone had cooked for him. When he and Tom had lived together he'd done all the cooking and he was used to cooking for one throughout his subsequent bachelor life-style. He hadn't minded, but Kayla's gesture tonight showed him how nice it was to have someone think of him, to want to take care of him for a change. It was also an indication that she was getting things under control her-self if she'd been able to juggle looking after Luke and making dinner. He certainly hadn't expected it.

'What have I done to deserve this?' Once he'd hung up his coat and walked through to the dining room he could see she'd gone all out for him.

The table was set for two, with heaped bowls of vegetable pasta. He was grateful she'd gone to this trouble for his benefit. In this case, the way to a man's heart was defi-nitely through his stomach. He'd thought he couldn't love her any more than he already did until she'd surprised him with this.

The thought struck him so hard he practically fell into his chair. He loved her, and not in the way he loved the look of this carb-laden meal before him. In the couldn't-stop-thinking-about-her, didn't-know-how-he'd-live-without-her conventional sense. He'd assumed his want of her company had arisen from being around her so much it had become a habit. Now they'd had a little time apart he could see it was much more than that. He wanted to spend every second of every day with her, raising their son, or kissing like teenagers in the first flush of love. Preferably both.

'I thought it would be nice for us to sit down to a meal together once you got home from work. Luke's getting settled into a routine now and things are becoming more manageable.' She certainly looked happier and he could see she'd taken time with her hair and clothes today. Not that he would've minded if she'd had bedhead and spent the day in her pyjamas. She simply appeared more like the Kayla he'd first met, so together and confident.

'It's great. Thank you. I mean, you didn't have to, but it's much appreciated.' He helped himself to a mouthful of creamy pasta and Jamie knew he'd found heaven here with her and Luke. There was nothing else he could've wanted for and he considered himself a very lucky man indeed.

'I can't guarantee it'll be a regular occurrence once I'm back to work.' Kayla was picking at her dinner whilst he was wolfing his down. Jamie hoped cooking this for him hadn't been a step too far for her.

'Of course. We can always take turns making dinner. I'm just happy to have some company. Usually I'm a dinner-for-one-in-front-of-the-TV sort, so anything else is a bonus.' When Luke was older meal times would become messier as he explored new foods and textures. They'd probably spend their evenings cleaning the evidence of it off the walls.

'I'm glad you're enjoying it.' She gave him an uneasy smile and laid her knife and fork down on her plate side by side. It looked as though she was preparing to tackle something more unsavoury to her palate. If Jamie hadn't almost finished eating he might've lost his appetite too at the thought they were going to have a talk about something more serious than dinner or assigning household chores.

'Okay, what's wrong?' He didn't actually want to know when he was content to carry on as they were. In asking they'd have to confront whatever was ailing her and the family dream might come crashing down around him. Except he'd promised to be honest with her and that didn't involve pretending there was nothing wrong when there was clearly a problem. In return, he'd expect Kayla to be honest with him.

'I'm thinking about returning to work.' She was chewing her bottom lip, but if she thought he was the type of partner to keep her chained to the kitchen she didn't know him at all. Similarly, he'd always known Kayla wouldn't be a housewife for ever. She had too much to give to be wasted on just one man.

'Good for you.' He wanted her to see he was being supportive and not to be afraid of saying whatever was on her mind. It was the only way to make a relationship work and, goodness knew, he wanted this one to last.

'You don't mind?'

'Not at all. Why should I? It's your decision, your life. I'm sure we can make some child-care arrangements for Luke around both of our jobs.' They'd be thorough in their search for suitable help in that area when neither of them would take chances when it came to doing what was best for their son.

'Actually, I was thinking about taking him with me to work.'

He took a minute to consider that extra in-formation. It could work. As a doula, Kayla worked for herself and, although that involved being on call for a patient going into labour, there was nothing stopping her from taking Luke too. It was preferable to leaving him with a stranger in a nursery.

'I'll be here to do my bit too and I can watch him if you get called out through the night.' He didn't want her to shut him out again or disrupt Luke's sleep merely to make a point that she could do everything herself.

'I was considering going back into midwifery.' It wasn't a huge bombshell, given the way she'd become immersed back into that role so suddenly yesterday.

However, he wished she would hit him with everything at once rather than drip-feeding him little titbits.

'How would that work with Luke? Do they have crèches for the hospital staff? Would you have to retake your qualifications after being away for so long?' It didn't matter to him if she did. He'd support her emotionally and financially until she was exactly where she needed to be to find her vocation.

'Not where I want to practise. I've been looking at helping out in the clinic Tom and Liam set up. Jamie, I want to go to Vietnam and take Luke with me.'

There it was, the devastating truth truck capable of obliterating everything in its path and leaving him with nothing. Kayla was leaving him and taking their son with her.

As she said it, she tried to focus on the excitement of a new adventure instead of the sadness at ending things with Jamie. She wanted to carry on with Liam and Tom's efforts and be someone her son could be proud of when he was older. As well as put some distance between her and Jamie to get her senses back in working order.

'No way in hell.' Jamie's voice was so measured and menacing it sounded so unlike him.

'Excuse me?' A prickling sensation started across her skin and crept up the back of her neck as she found he was no longer a caring partner supporting her, but a stern authority figure dictating to her. It gave her flashbacks of Paul telling her she wouldn't go out with her friends if she really loved him. Then her father, spittle forming at the corners of his mouth as he went nose to nose to yell at her when she'd expressed an interest in a school disco.

'I'm sorry, Kayla, but there is no way you are taking my son to another country. To the very place where my brother died. I didn't know you could be so cruel.' That hard look she'd seen on his face when she'd broached the subject had now changed into one of pain. He was thinking only of himself by accusing her of such venom. Not of what she wanted or of the good she could do where it would count most.

It said a lot that in the heat of the discussion he only cared about his son being taken away, not that she would be leaving too. Clearly, she'd been reading way too much into those passionate interludes between them.

'If you think so little of me I can see there is no future for us.' It had all been too good to be true. She'd have been better off as that cynical version of herself, combatting his attempts to charm her, when she'd known things would end this way. They always did. Thanks to her parents she attracted people who thought they could rule over her the way they had. Except this time she had Luke to think about. He was her priority and he'd be safer travelling with her than being stuck in a toxic house like the one she'd grown up in. She wasn't going to wait around until the full force of Jamie's dominance made itself known and he tried to impose it on Luke too.

'I live in the real world. One full of everyday dangers for a newborn without asking for more by taking him to a foreign country.'

'Do you honestly think I would risk my son's well-being?' She couldn't believe what she was hearing. He was being ridiculous. It wasn't as though she wouldn't have researched the idea thoroughly before deeming it safe to travel with a baby. No, Jamie was trying to assert his authority over her, and over their son. She wasn't having it.

'That's exactly what you're doing.' He pushed back his chair and got up to pace around the room. Determined not to be intimidated ever again, she copied his move, pulling herself up to her full height to face him.

'Luke is my son. Liam was my brother. This decision is mine to make.' Her independence meant more to her than a possible romance that had been doomed from the start. She'd gone ahead with the surrogacy idea at the time because she'd believed having a child in an actual relationship wasn't going to be possible. There was no joy in finding out she'd been right all along. The biggest mistake she'd made was adding his name to the birth certificate.

'It's not all about you, Kayla. Luke is my son too and, in case you'd forgotten, I also lost a brother. Which is the reason I'm not prepared to let you risk my son's life over there.'

Her hands balled into fists into his use of that word, which conjured up memories of her parents' lists of rules and the consequences she incurred if she broke any of them. Thank goodness Jamie didn't have any real hold over her other than the grip he had around her heart. At least seeing his true colours now should lessen the heartbreak she was facing at losing him.

'If I hadn't already made my mind up about going, your attitude has convinced me why this is a good idea. I need to get away and re-member who I am. That's no longer a woman who'll cower every time someone raises their voice at me.'

He actually laughed at that. The dark, hol-low sound giving her chills. 'Kayla, I am nothing like your parents. I care. That's why I don't want you going over there.'

She wanted to believe him, and she had, up until a few minutes ago. Now those barriers had shot back up there was no way she was going to let him sweet-talk his way back into her heart and take advantage of her. 'I'm sorry, Jamie, but my mind is made up. We're not going for ever but, make no mistake about it, we are going.'

His face darkened. 'Not if I can help it.'

She didn't like the threat hovering in the tense atmosphere, waiting for the opportunity to strike and hit her where it could do the most damage. 'What do you mean?'

'As Luke's father I have certain rights. I'll fight you on this if I have to.'

The thing she'd dreaded most about their crazy situation had actually come into being. Jamie was going to betray her in the worst possible way. He was going to use that trust she'd shown him in naming him on the birth certificate to try and control what happened to her son.

'You will have to. There is no way on this

earth I'm going to give him up. He's all I have in the world.' She hated the sound of her strangled voice as she battled not to cry in front of him. It was a sign of weakness she couldn't afford to show him when he'd probably try and use it against her somehow.

'Be reasonable, Kayla.' He walked towards her, arms outstretched, but she didn't want him to touch her now she realised everything between them had been a lie. All along he'd only wanted access to his son and used her to get it. She'd been so weak, so desperate for someone to love her and fill that void in her life that Liam's death had left, she'd abandoned her senses to believe they could be together as a family. Now she knew the truth she had to fight to save what was left of it. Her and Luke.

'You're the one who's being unreasonable, Jamie. All I want to do is take Luke to the place which meant so much to his uncles, the men who were supposed to raise him. Without them he would never have been born. You didn't even want him, remember?'

'That's not fair. He wasn't a baby then.

Since his birth you know I've been there every step of the way for you both.'

'Until now.'

'All I'm asking is that you think about what you're doing to Luke, and to me, by going through with this harebrained scheme.' He was back to being that arrogant know-it-all she'd met at the wedding. This was the true face of Jamie Garrett and the supportive partner had obviously been a ruse to garner her trust. He hadn't shown any interest in hearing her plans or what safety measures she'd have in place to protect Luke out there. As far as he was concerned, his word was law and he wouldn't hear any different. So why should she even give him house room?

'Get out of my house, Jamie.' She didn't often raise her voice so when she did people took notice. They knew she was serious.

'Pardon me?' He didn't budge.

'I said get out of my house.' She marched down the hall, lifted his bag and his coat, opened the front door and chucked them out onto the path.

'Kayla, please.' He followed her but hovered in the doorway, unwilling to go after his belongings.

'You can collect the rest of your things tomorrow. I'll box them up.' Arms folded, jaw set, she was unyielding in her decision. She needed him gone so she'd no longer be under his influence. So her feelings for him wouldn't eat away at her conscience until she doubted her own decision-making.

'I thought we'd already had the row over the house. It's half mine too.' It was a last-ditch attempt to guilt her into letting him stay but nothing could persuade her to change her mind now. She had too much to lose.

'Yeah? Sue me. When you're talking to your solicitor about custody rights you can bring it up with him. Goodbye, Jamie.' She held the door open wider for him, refusing to back down.

'Kayla...you know I don't want any of this.'

'Goodnight, Jamie.'

He sighed and shook his head before eventually stepping outside. She slammed the door, not wanting to see him stoop to retrieve his things from the ground and so that he couldn't see the tears running in rivers down her cheeks. It was the hardest thing she'd ever had to do and she only found the strength because of her son. She was Luke's mother and, unlike her own parents, would protect him at all costs. Even if it cost her the love of her life.

CHAPTER ELEVEN

'Where are Mrs Henshaw's blood results? We've been waiting weeks now. It's unacceptable. Get onto the lab.' Jamie was at the clinic early, catching up on the patients the locum had treated in his absence.

'What's wrong with you this morning? Did the little one keep you up all night?' When his secretary didn't immediately rush to follow his instructions he eventually looked up from his computer screen.

'Sorry. What?' If she'd been trying to start a conversation with him he'd missed it. His head was full of thoughts only about Kayla and Luke and how much of a mess he'd made of things last night.

'You're not your usual affable self. I thought perhaps the baby had kept you awake.' She was subtly pointing out he was being a grouch. His personal life was not something his patients, or the staff, should suffer for. The only one to blame was him for his outburst at Kayla last night. As a result, he'd spent the rest of the night, alone in his bed, cursing himself for ruining the best thing that had ever happened to him.

'Er…something like that.' He had to say something to get rid of her before she asked any more questions and it became obvious to her too what an idiot he'd been.

It was natural for Kayla to want to go and see what Liam and Tom had been working towards out in Vietnam. Any sane person would have been proud that she wanted to do more than go sightseeing and intended to put her medical knowledge to use out there. Deep down he knew she'd never put Luke in danger either. He'd panicked the instant she'd suggested the trip, thinking of all the problems that could befall the people he loved most in the world.

Looking back today, he thought it was no wonder she'd thrown him out. He hadn't asked anything about the trip she was planning, focusing only on the negatives. Telling her he'd fight for custody had sealed the fate of their relationship. It had been a stupid thing to say. Done in the heat of the moment before he'd taken the time to think about what he was saying. Jamie wished he could take it back, but he doubted he'd get the chance. He'd be lucky if the rest of his belongings weren't strewn all around the garden by the time he got over to the house tonight.

'Right, then. I guess I'll go and chase up some results.' Perhaps sensing she wasn't going to get any more conversation out of him, his secretary scooped up the paperwork and scurried out of the room to find better company.

'Good idea.' He didn't look up to see her leave. To be honest he'd been so caught up in feeling sorry for himself he'd forgotten she was there. Nothing seemed to hold his attention at present. He'd lost interest in everything because he had nothing without Kayla and Luke.

His hand hovered over the phone sitting on the desk. He wanted to hear her voice, ask how Luke was this morning, and most of all apologise for his overreaction. Except he knew that fear something would happen to them out there wouldn't leave him. There was no guarantee they wouldn't go around in circles disagreeing over her plans. He didn't know how to resolve the situation, only that he wanted to. They had so much together, had a future before them, and he didn't want to throw that away. If only he knew how to keep Kayla happy and Luke safe.

Right now, he'd settle for a conversation without Kayla thinking about the harsh treatment she'd received at the hands of her parents. He knew that was why she'd been so defensive and angry enough to throw him out. She couldn't despise him more than he despised himself for making that comparison a possibility in her eyes. He'd never intentionally hurt her, but he didn't know if it was too late to convince her of that. If he told her he loved her, wanted to be with her for ever, she wouldn't believe him because of the timing. It was down to him to find some way to convince her they had something worth saving and do everything within his power to make that happen.

'I take it things didn't go well?' Cherry was on the phone first thing in the morning. It only took Kayla's sniffling when she answered the phone for her to realise things hadn't gone to plan.

'That's an understatement. Please don't say you told me so.' She'd spent enough time berating herself for being so stupid in trusting Jamie, for falling for him, and making him such an important part of her and Luke's lives in the first place.

'Oh, Kayla, I would never do that. I just didn't want to see you hurt like this.' Thank goodness her friend *couldn't* see her. She'd have taken one look at Kayla's puffy eyes and red nose and tracked Jamie down to give him a piece of her mind. Doulas, and best friends, were very protective of new mums and their somewhat fragile emotions.

'Well, it's done now. Jamie made it clear he's going to fight for custody if I try and take

Luke abroad.' As she said the words that sadness that had been sitting heavily on her chest from last night again threatened to suffocate her. It was one thing walking away from her parents, who had never shown her any kind of love, but quite another to leave someone she loved. It was heartbreaking, knowing it was the end for them. Even more so to think it had all been a lie.

She took no pleasure in discovering she'd been right to be wary of getting in too deep. Now she was questioning if he'd ever had feelings for her at all, beyond her being the mother of his child. Although she'd never said it, never admitted it to herself, she'd fallen in love with Jamie. That was why it was hurting so damn much to have lost him. Now she was grieving all over again for a man she loved and a life she'd never have. How difficult it was going to be to still have him in her life as Luke's father and be reminded of everything that had happened between them.

'There's no hope at all?' The sympathy in Cherry's voice was all it took to set Kayla off again, tears falling and her throat constricting, strangling the wail rising from the depths of her soul.

'No,' she croaked. 'Things were said which can never be forgotten.'

'That's a shame. I mean, I knew he wouldn't like the idea, but I thought you could work it out, talk it through. You two seemed a good fit.'

Life had a horrible way of surprising her when she least suspected it.

'Thank goodness we didn't do anything stupid like get married or I'd be in real trouble. No, it's better to end things now before it gets too complicated.' If she'd agreed to him moving in permanently she would've been forced to see him every day, take him into account in every decision she made. At least this way she could try and forget him and retain some of her independence.

'What about your trip?'

'Oh, don't worry, it's still going ahead. With or without Jamie's consent.' That stubborn streak that had flourished in her since her move to London, away from her parents' influence, stopped her tears in their tracks. She would find a way to take this trip with Luke. Even if she had to steal away in the dead of night. No one was going to stop her from living her own life.

When Cherry heard that she grew more concerned about Kayla's state of mind and she had to talk her out of rushing over. She was done being weak. The one thing she did draw strength from was her son, so as soon as she hung up on Cherry she rushed upstairs to get him.

'Morning, sleepyhead.' She had to rouse Luke for his morning feed. If she let him sleep on he'd be awake all night and, goodness knew, she didn't want to go back to that again.

He didn't really stir even when she lifted him out of his crib. It was so unlike him. Usually he was wriggling about in there, his arms and legs flailing around, eager to get out and start the day. This morning he was just kind of floppy. Call it experience, or plain old motherly instinct, but she knew something was wrong.

'Luke? Come on, wake up, sweetheart.' She

tried blowing gently on his face, but he wasn't responding. His chest was rising and falling steadily so she knew he was still breathing. A huge relief when she considered the alternative.

His cheeks were bright red and when she felt his forehead he was burning up. He was too young to be teething and, though it could be something as simple as a virus, running a fever at this age could cause lasting problems. She laid him down on her bed and stripped him down to try and reduce his temperature, but she didn't want to take any chances. If this was anyone else's baby she would've told them not to panic, it probably wasn't anything serious, but to get him checked out with the GP as soon as possible.

Calculating the length of time it would take to get him over to the health centre, she decided she wanted more immediate action. She grabbed her phone from the bedside table and contemplated who to call. It was an emergency to her, but she wasn't convinced a temperature necessitated an ambulance. There was only one person she knew who could help and who would be as concerned for Luke's welfare. She had to swallow her pride and put her son before her wounded heart.

At the sound of Kayla's voice on the phone Jamie had almost broken down and begged for forgiveness there and then. It had been the fear in her voice and the reason for her call that had stopped him. She wasn't extending an olive branch, she was contacting him because their son was ill. He hadn't wasted any time in leaving work and jumping in his car. There was nothing more important to him than Luke's health.

'How is he?' He was breathless when he got to the house. Kayla had come to the door with Luke in her arms. She was pale, apart from the redness around her eyes, and it was all he could do not to reach out and hug her, assure her everything was going to be all right.

'I'm probably being one of those over-anxious mums, but I didn't want to take any chances. He wasn't himself at all this morning and running a temperature.'

'Not at all. Better to be safe than sorry.

Thanks for phoning me.' She could've contacted her GP, or turned to Cherry for help, but she'd chosen him. He was thankful that she wasn't letting their disagreement come between him and his son. Hopefully it was an indication that, no matter what their relationship, he would still be part of the family.

'Where would you like me to examine him?' It seemed so odd now to be asking permission to go anywhere in the house when it had become his home up until last night, but he wasn't here as Kayla's estranged partner. He didn't want to upset her any more by asserting his rights to the house and his son. That was a matter that could be resolved at a later date and hopefully through a civilised discussion.

'We can take him upstairs. I'm sorry I dragged you away from work, but I thought you would understand my worry more than anyone.' She gave him a sad smile before leading him up to her bedroom. A place where they'd spent so many nights together ensuring their son had everything he needed.

'Of course I do. As for work, I wasn't supposed to be back until next week, so I think I'm surplus to requirements for the time being. They were glad to get rid of me for a while.' He thought back to earlier, when his secretary had all but accused him of being a pain to be around. Then the relief he'd seen on her face when he'd said he had to leave. He vowed to make it up to her for being so grumpy. Cake seemed to be the required currency to get the staff on side and he made the decision to stop by the bakery on his way to work tomorrow. He couldn't afford to upset all the people in his life.

Once upstairs, Kayla laid Luke on the bed. She'd done the right thing in stripping him down and trying to lower his temperature. Unchecked, a fever could lead to fitting and a possibility of leaving a child brain-damaged. Jamie tried not to think the worst. They were both medical professionals; they weren't going to let their child get into that sort of danger.

'His temperature is still high.'

Kayla leaned over and studied the reading for herself. 'It is lower than it was first thing.'

'Good. I'll check his ears too.' With his otoscope, he shone a light into Luke's ears. 'There's a lot of inflammation there. I think he's got an ear infection.'

'My poor lamb.' Kayla sat on the bed and did her best to console her son, who was protesting against the intrusion.

'I'll nip out and get him some ear drops to try and take that swelling down. He might need some antibiotics too if it doesn't clear up.' All being well, they could get this under control. He knew both of them could relax if Luke's temperature would come down and they could relieve some of his pain. At least there was something he could do in this situation to stop him from feeling so powerless. It was relations between him and Kayla that still needed attending to. He wasn't going to sit back and let resentment steal away what they'd had before he'd opened his big mouth, when they had so much worth saving.

Since the lines of communication had been opened, Jamie hoped Kayla would hear him out on the other matter tearing his guts out. This was his only chance to convince her he was not the monster she believed him to be and he would do everything in his power to prove it.

Kayla had stopped fretting so much since Jamie had dropped everything and rushed over. Not only because he'd gone out and got the medical supplies needed to treat Luke. Despite everything that had been said, all the things she'd accused him of last night, she was glad to have him back here. He'd been the only person she'd wanted to come and treat Luke and reassure her. Underneath it all she knew he was nothing like her parents. She'd been looking for an excuse to push him away because it was easier to do that than to risk her heart. Scarred so deeply by the past, she was afraid there could be no such thing as a happy family for her and didn't want to put herself through the pain of losing everything when it all went wrong. Except in the aftermath of that conversation last night, pain was all she'd felt. There had been no relief in sending Jamie away because he'd challenged her decisions.

'Do you mind if I stay here until I know he's out of the woods?' Jamie had returned from the chemist within record time. Now he'd administered the ear drops and given Luke some liquid paracetamol to help bring his temperature down, all they could do was watch and wait. Kayla was lying right here beside him on the bed until she knew he was all right.

'Not at all.' She knew Jamie was equally anxious. He wouldn't have dropped everything to come here if he weren't.

He glanced at the bed uncertainly as he took off his coat.

'Go ahead. Take off your shoes first, though.' She gave him a little smile to show she didn't mind him lying here with them. After all, it had become commonplace for all three of them to end up in here. It would be churlish now to deny him that closeness to his son.

'Thanks.' He kicked off his shoes, removed his tie and opened the top button of his shirt. It reminded her of that day in the park when they'd been so content, carefree, and unbothered by the world around them.

'I'm not going to change my mind about the trip, Jamie.' It was one thing deferring to him when Luke was sick, but she wanted him to realise it wouldn't change her plans. She wasn't going to allow him to use an ear infection to take the higher moral ground.

'I wouldn't expect anything less.' He was lying on his side grinning at her, back to being his irritating self when she was trying to be serious. They couldn't simply forget the one thing guaranteed to tear them apart even if there was a chance to get back together.

'I mean, if anything, this goes to prove he can get sick anywhere, but we'll have the same medicines available out there as we have here. That's the whole point of the clinic.' Childhood illness was part of life and they weren't going to do Luke any favours by trying to wrap him in cotton wool. Being Jamie Garrett's son didn't mean he should be treated any differently from any other child.

'I know.' The fact he wasn't putting up any argument only succeeded in her strengthening hers.

'You can't tell me how to live my life,

Jamie. I've had enough of that.' If he was agreeing with her only to secure a place in Luke's life, she knew he'd eventually break cover. 'I won't have Luke exposed to the sort of parent I was forced to suffer under.'

That did wipe the grin off his face and she braced herself for another altercation with Jamie's Mr Hyde alter ego. He shifted position so he was sitting upright.

'Do you honestly believe I am anything like your parents? That I would prefer to keep you trained to obey my every command rather than have you fighting me on every issue?' His scowl had softened as he tilted his head to question her real perception of him.

She thought back to those times when they'd clashed, the reasons behind it, and the passion it had sparked between them. Most times it had been at her instigation, fighting her feelings for him, yet unable to resist the pull between them. Jamie had always seemed to enjoy it, her quest for independence and spiky defences not putting him off. He'd never asked her to be anything but true to herself.

'No,' she answered quietly.

'No. I love you, Kayla. I love Luke. The only thing I'm guilty of is wanting to keep you safe. I know I went about it the wrong way but there was no deeper, darker motive for the way I acted last night.'

Her head was spinning. His words were going around and around too fast to catch hold of and really explore what he was saying. She closed her eyes, tried to make them slow down.

It was possible she'd sabotaged any chance of a relationship herself by insisting she was going to Vietnam now when there wasn't any real hurry. She'd simply been using it as an excuse to get away and avoid facing the feelings she had for him. Worried he didn't reciprocate them. He'd just said he loved her. It was why she was so afraid to invite him into her life. Loving Jamie was handing over a very big part of herself to him—her heart—and trusting him not to abuse the privilege.

It would be down to her whether or not to give him a second chance. That meant taking a leap of faith and trusting that he only had her and Luke's best interests at heart. There was only one way of testing that and remaining true to herself.

'I—I love you too, Jamie, but I'm still taking that trip. With Luke.' It took all the courage she had to tell him that and show him her weakness, but she couldn't expect honesty from Jamie and not give it in return.

'I thought you might say that. That's why I got these.' He pulled out a cardboard sleeve from his back pocket and handed it to her. When she opened it, there were tickets with their names on them nestled inside.

'What's this?'

'Airline vouchers. For all of us. I didn't know when, or how long you wanted to go for. You can use these whenever you're ready. I hope that's okay?'

'Er...yeah.' She pulled out the ticket with Jamie's name on it. 'You're coming too?'

'If you want me to? I'm never going to stop you doing anything you want to do. I want to be supportive. This can be our first family holiday.'

'I would really love that.' This gesture was everything, proving she didn't need to flee her feelings for him when he loved her and wanted to be by her side come what may.

'Wait. You're actually agreeing with me on something?'

'Yeah. Don't get too used to it. If I think something's worth fighting you on I won't hold back.'

'Oh, I'm counting on it. They do say the making up after is always the best part.' Jamie leaned over their sleeping baby with that devilish look in his eyes that told her she was in trouble. She kind of liked it.

'Really? Then we have some major making up to do.' She leaned over to meet him.

'Am I forgiven, then?'

'Shut up and kiss me, Jamie Garrett.'

'I'll take that as a yes, then,' he muttered against her lips before showing her exactly why she should forgive him. His kisses were worth risking her heart on.

Kayla had everything she needed in this

room. Her family. It might not be the one she'd planned for, but she knew Liam and Tom would be proud of them. Luke had two parents who loved him and that was all that mattered. Falling in love was just a bonus.

EPILOGUE

Two weeks later

'FLIGHTS AND ACCOMMODATION are booked. I have work covered until we come back. I know it might be premature since the trip isn't until the end of the year, but I want to make sure everything's in place. Is there anything else we might have forgotten?'

'I don't think so. If we have there's plenty of time to sort it out. Relax, Jamie.' Kayla couldn't help but laugh at his enthusiasm now they were going together as a family to Vietnam.

If she'd had any lingering doubts he was only going to keep her in check and make sure Luke wasn't in any danger, they'd vanished. He was taking his role as medical relief very seriously, liaising with the other staff out at the clinic to see what was needed.

Since he'd surprised her with the vouchers and they'd stopped bickering about the trip, life had been a dream for her. Luke had recovered from his ear infection after a couple of days and she'd asked Jamie to move in permanently to prove the faith she was putting in him as a father and a partner.

He was still sleeping in his own room, but he hadn't put her under any pressure to share her bed. If anything, it was she who was suffering when they stopped things from going any further than lingering kisses and he retired to the other end of the hallway. She didn't want them to be in separate rooms in Vietnam but wanted them to go out there united in every way.

'I will once we get this one to bed.' Jamie scooped up their son and carried him into the nursery. Luke had settled better in his cot there with more room to move around. Although they'd both been anxious about leaving him to sleep on his own there, baby monitors had been able to reassure them he was fine.

When Jamie came back she knew she would

have to make the move because he would never presume to share her bed. After tonight, she hoped that would change.

'You don't have to go.' It didn't come out as confident or as sultry as the invitation had sounded in her head.

'Are you sure?' If his raised eyebrows were anything to go by, he hadn't expected the offer either.

'I'm sure.' She patted the side of the bed he usually lay on when they were here cuddling with Luke.

'I don't want you to feel you have to do anything...' He was sliding onto the covers beside her, close enough she could feel his warm breath on her face.

'I want to. It's been a while though.' Only now, when they were lying here together, was she beginning to worry. Now she'd had a baby, her body wasn't the same. Never mind the addition of stretchmarks, she didn't know if things would *feel* the same down there.

'We'll take it one step at a time.' He followed the promise with one of those long, languid kisses capable of making her forget her own name.

She quivered with anticipation as he slid his hand under her nightdress, up along her thigh before slipping in between her legs. Tentatively, he tested her readiness with his fingers, but she'd never wanted anyone or anything more. As he stroked her she let her head fall back onto the pillow, enjoying the sensation of getting to know her own body again and what she liked.

The sheets rustled, and she opened her eyes to see Jamie moving down the bed.

'What—?'

'Shh.' He quieted her with that mischievous glint in his eye as he nudged her legs apart and his intent became clear.

Kayla was gasping for air before he even touched her. Then he dotted gossamer-light kisses along her inner thigh and she heard herself groaning for more. He parted her with his tongue and the rush of arousal coursing through her left her limp in its wake. His intimate caresses brought her a pleasure she'd never dreamed of, until he began to thrust into her with his tongue and he exceeded those new heights. She was floating on a cloud of ecstasy at his command, in no hurry to wrest back control of her body this time.

There was no holding back as he drove her to the brink of her climax and when she toppled over the edge she fell hard.

When she was able to breathe properly again, think and talk, she realised she was the only one who'd had any relief. 'What about you, Jamie? It's not fair to leave you wanting.'

He kissed the tip of her nose. 'Don't worry about me. There's plenty of time for us to explore each other. A lifetime, if you can put up with me.'

'Sounds like heaven to me.' It wasn't a conventional proposal but, then again, they had never been a conventional family.

Kayla wouldn't have had it any other way.

* * * * *

LET'S TALK

Romance

For exclusive extracts, competitions
and special offers, find us online:

f facebook.com/millsandboon

⊙ @millsandboonuk

🐦 @millsandboon

Or get in touch on 0844 844 1351*

For all the latest titles coming soon,
visit millsandboon.co.uk/nextmonth

*Calls cost 7p per minute plus your phone company's price per
minute access charge